SIX IMPOSSIBLE THINGS

SIX IMPOSSIBLE THINGS by FIONA WOOD

poppy

Little, Brown and Company
New York   Boston

Copyright © 2010 by Fiona Wood
Excerpt from *Wildlife* copyright © 2013 by Fiona Wood

Poppy

Hachette Book Group
1290 Avenue of the Americas, New York, NY 10104
Visit us at lb-teens.com

Poppy is an imprint of Little, Brown and Company.
The Poppy name and logo are trademarks of Hachette Book Group, Inc.

The publisher is not responsible for websites (or their content) that are not owned by the publisher.

"She Walks in Beauty," George Gordon, Lord Byron, 1815
"The Rime of the Ancient Mariner," Samuel Taylor Coleridge, 1798

The title *Six Impossible Things* is from an exchange between Alice and the White Queen in Lewis Carroll's *Through the Looking-Glass*.

First U.S. Edition: August 2015
First published in 2010 by Pan Macmillan Australia Pty, Ltd.

Library of Congress Cataloging-in-Publication Data

Wood, Fiona (Fiona Anna).
Six impossible things / by Fiona Wood. — First U.S. edition.
pages cm
"Poppy."
Summary: Fourteen-year-old Dan Cereill's life is turned upside-down when his father announces he is gay and leaves Dan and his mother with nothing, forcing them to move to an aunt's house, Dan to enroll in public school, and his mother to try to start a business, but the top thing on Dan's list is kissing Estelle, the girl next door.
ISBN 978-0-316-24216-5 (hc) — ISBN 978-0-316-24217-2 (ebook) [1. Moving, Household—Fiction. 2. Family problems—Fiction. 3. Interpersonal relations—Fiction. 4. High schools—Fiction. 5. Schools—Fiction. 6. Gay fathers—Fiction. 7. Australia—Fiction.] I. Title.
PZ7.W84925Six 2015 [Fic]—dc23 2014017241

10 9 8 7 6 5 4 3 2 1

RRD-C

Printed in the United States of America

For Zoe and George

PROLOGUE

There's this girl I know.

I know her by heart. I know her in every way but one: actuality.

Her name is Estelle. I yearn for her.

She walks in beauty—yes, like the night of cloudless climes and starry skies—with one iPod earbud in at all times—the sound track of her life.

She's stopped biting her nails, except for the left hand little finger.

She sometimes nibbles the inside seam of her school sweater cuffs.

She's an only child. Like me.

She plays the cello.

She likes mochaccinos. And banana milkshakes—made with syrup, not real bananas. And chocolate—especially Cherry Ripe bars. She has a friend in New York she sends Cherry Ripes to. You can't buy them there.

She has more than one friend. Unlike me.

She lives next door. To where we live now.

She laughs a lot.

She and I have a three-band overlap in our top five bands.

Her favorite writers are Georgette Heyer and J. D. Salinger.

I can't tell you how I know all this stuff about someone I haven't met.

1

If you can forget that it means someone just died, inheriting something is a good thing, isn't it? A stroke of luck. Improved circumstances. But when it happened to us, it had the opposite effect. Everything got a whole lot worse. Quickly.

Things had been going wrong at my father's work. Even in a place the size of ours, I could hear the fights. Our apparently comfortable life was an illusion propped up by some massive overdraft. It was all about to come tumbling down. And we to come tumbling after.

Money problems were just the beginning. Listening in from the upstairs landing one night, I understood in a single sick thud of my heart that my parents didn't even seem to like each other anymore. But since when? Smiiiiiile! That's us. We *look* happy. Suspended on the Brooklyn Bridge; eating falafels in the Marais in Paris; underwater with blue-lipped clams off Green Island...

What went wrong? When? And how did I not notice?

Was I like that frog not realizing the water's getting hotter till it's too late and he's soup?

When my mother's great-aunt Adelaide died and left her a house, I thought it might take some pressure off the situation. And it did, but not in the way I hoped. It was about a nanosecond later that my father dropped the bombshell— the family business was in the hands of receivers, he had been declared bankrupt, he was gay, and he was moving out.

Guys, please, one life-changing shock at a time, I felt like saying.

There was a mortgagee's auction of our house. That's when the bank sells you up because it basically owns the house. The creditors, people to whom my father owed money, sent in liquidators, who came and took all our stuff away. It's pretty much like moving, only you never see the moving truck again.

Josh Whitters from school pulled up on his bike when the truck was being loaded.

"See you're moving, Cereill," he said.

"Your powers of observation are impeccable, Whitters." I wondered if he knew the whole sorry story.

"Hear your dad's gone broke."

He knew.

"Yep."

"Loser."

He took off.

I'm almost sure he didn't see them load my Teenage Mutant Ninja Turtles beanbag chair. I know, I should have given it away years ago.

Usually in a business meltdown like this one, people get to keep their personal stuff, but in our case, every single thing we had was owned by the company.

My mother and I had stashed some stuff at her friend Alice's house—kitchen things, books, clothes, my comics, and a TV. And we've kept the photos, but not the silver frames. Our entire life in a couple of boxes.

The liquidators went through the place like a plague of locusts. It was horrible walking through the empty house. I hadn't heard that echo-y sound since we moved in. Back then it sounded like excitement and things to find out. Now it just sounded like The End and stuff I wished I didn't know.

We'd been uprooted. Liquidated. Terminated. Not to mention deserted. Whitters was right. I sure felt like a loser.

2

The list:

1. Kiss Estelle. I know. I haven't met her. Technically. But it gets top spot regardless.
2. Get a job. We're in a complete mess financially. It's down to me to tide us over moneywise if my mother's new business crashes.
3. Cheer my mother up. Better chance of business not crashing if she's half okay.
4. It's not like I expect to be cool or popular at the new school, but I'm going to try not to be a complete nerd/loser.

5. Should talk to my father when he calls. But how, when the only thing I want to ask is something I can't bear to hear the answer to: How could you leave us like this?

6. The existential one. Figure out how to be good. I don't want to become the sort of person who up and leaves his family out of the blue.

Impossible.
Impossible.
Impossible.
Impossible.
Impossible.
Impossible.

3

Waking up, it's never more than a couple of seconds before it washes back over me, what's real. Wham. A sucker punch to the gut—anger sits there with an evil grin. Misery is beside it, weighing me down like a brick. Three weeks since my dad left and my mother and I moved into her great-aunt Adelaide's house. Former great-aunt. It's freezing here. Mid-year holidays; the depth of winter. My fingers are so cold I can't make a fist.

The windows have to stay open because of the smell. Heaters are emergency-use-only, because of finances. The only time I thaw out is in bed, and it takes ages, because the world of electric blankets is past tense.

There are six bedrooms here, including the one Adelaide

actually died in. That door stays shut. Choosing my room was easy; I went for the one that stinks least. I've been spending a whole lot of time in bed since we moved in. It's like my body is telling me to hibernate, and I'm listening. It should make for a riveting essay on what I did in the school holidays.

It turns out that we don't even *own* this house, either. What my mother has inherited is a lifetime *use* of the house. When she dies, it goes to the Historic Homes Trust, not to me.

So if she dies anytime soon, I'm on the streets. Or back with my father. I guess that'd force us onto speaking terms, at least. Pity she can't sell the house. It'd be worth heaps. I've checked out the window of the local real estate agent.

To make the inheritance even more oddball, there's some guy who gets to live out back, in the old stables building. That's in the will, too, apparently. We haven't met him yet. He's away.

My mother's not exactly thrilled with the arrangement. But it's like she says, at least we've got a roof over our heads. Which is more than we would've had. We don't have a cent left. We won't even have a car when the lease runs out at the end of the month.

As if we could afford to fill it up with petrol, anyway.

There was a chance that Adelaide might have left my mother some cash, but no such luck. She left her money to the National Gallery, which I doubt needs it as much as we do.

The only thing the lawyer handed over when we went to see him was a black—ebony—jewelry box. My mother's eyes lit up, but I could see the lawyer felt apologetic. So I knew she wouldn't find what she was rummaging for.

"Who got the diamonds?" she asked finally.

"A local shopkeeper."

"That'd be right," my mother said.

The box contained glass beads—clear with white streaks—a wooden spool of orange thread, some cardboard train tickets, nine small gold safety pins, a few copper one- and two-cent coins, and a handful of little carved insects and animals.

"I believe these had sentimental value?" he asked, sympathy leaking from his pinstripes.

My mother smiled. "I played with them when I was little. I used to line them up along the windowsill."

Good times. Thank god I wasn't a kid back then.

The lawyer cleared his throat, fiddled with a cuff, and snuck a look at his watch. No doubt he had other clients out there awaiting disappointment.

"Would you be interested in contesting the will?" he asked. .

"Certainly not. Adelaide had a perfectly sound mind."

The lawyer looked quietly pleased. You wouldn't think so, because it would've meant more money for him, but I could tell he thought my mother's response was honorable. So did I.

We get to keep the dog, too. Howard. Though strictly speaking, on the inheritance ledger, that's a minus because we have to feed him.

Being honorable obviously didn't stop my mother from feeling pissed off. I had to remind her to slow down on the way home. We can't exactly afford traffic fines these days. And, yes, we're in the deep end without a floatie, but I'm pretty sure neither of us wants to die just yet. She was making a scary growling noise between clenched teeth.

"Do you want to talk?" I asked. Obviously hoping the answer would be no.

"Talk, ha! I just don't know what the point is, Dan," she said. I sensed she meant point of life, existence, etc., rather than point of talking. Clearly a bit of life-coach action was required. Not really in my skill set, unfortunately.

"Well—I guess there's always the old glass half full... isn't there?"

"That really only works if there's actually something in the glass," she said. "We, sadly, are in a glass-empty situation."

"There's the house."

"Yes, the house. A mausoleum, certainly, but I suppose it's better than the street."

Stress level: extreme. It's like she was a jar with the lid screwed on too tight, and inside the jar were pickles, angry pickles, and they were fermenting, and about to explode.

"What are you thinking about?" she asked.

"Lunch."

She groaned. Better than the growl.

Better than the street. Better than the growl. Things actually could be worse. But not much.

Where we live now is the exact middle in a row of five houses. It's a massive two-story Victorian Gothic terrace. The front facade forms a point over each house as though the top has been trimmed with giant pinking shears. There's a brick-pillared balcony on each first floor and mean little gargoyles leaning on their elbows, jeering and grimacing in the dip of each zig. It's in a book about Australian architecture—this actual building. They call it a "significant exemplar." It's grim—the sort of place you could set a horror film. Its red bricks are blackened with time, or pollution, or both, I guess.

Moving in took all of about five minutes.

I saw Estelle for the first time that day.

Invisible behind sheer curtains, I stood in the bay window at the front of the house wishing to be anywhere but there, wishing it were two months ago and I had a mutant power that let me change the course of history, when she walked up the street, dreaming, completely unaware of the seismic shifts in my heart she was creating with each step.

She stopped outside our place and stared up into the bare branches of the sidewalk plane tree. First checking there was no one nearby, she turned slowly around and around and around, framing her view of the twig-snaggled sky with a hand held to her eye.

Then she walked into the house next door, half dizzy, smiling, and carrying my heart.

There's this sky she likes.

4

That was the last day of term, and we've been here for the whole holidays.

This is what I've been doing:

1. Sleeping—like I already said.
2. Trying to catch another glimpse of Estelle. Several sightings. No meetings.
3. Getting to know Howard. Enigmatic Howard. All-knowing Howard. Long looks. Doesn't say much.
4. Listening to my mother's part in phone conversations with my father about me.
5. Worrying about them, and about the new school, and—to take my mind off those things...

6. Following the Historic Homes Trust people around while they catalog the house's contents.

I could tell the furniture guy, Bryce, was annoyed, but Posy, who did glass and porcelain, was nice. By the end, her sympathy was worse than him being pissed off. She'd ask me what my plans were for the day as she checked underneath things and made notes like "pair of first-period Worcester plates." It was awkward for both of us when the answer was always "not much"—i.e., nothing.

Sometime deep into the second week, when the comment about how it was too bad it wasn't summer so I could go to the Fitzroy Baths had worn right through, she said, "Joining a club can be a good way to get to know people, Dan. What do you like doing?"

"Reading. Mostly."

I wanted to make her feel better, so I added, "There's chess. Only I don't like people who like chess. Not the ones I've met anyway."

On her last day, when every item in the house had been cataloged, tagged, coded, and insured, she casually mentioned the Kids' Help Line.

"There's no problem that can't be helped by talking about it. At your age sometimes things can seem worse than they are..."

I sighed. "Things aren't great, but it's not like I'm suicidal. And I do have a friend—he'll be back soon."

Maybe you're lucky if you've got one friend.

Mine—Fred—is staying with his mother these holidays. She's living in London for six months, in Chelsea, studying Georgian underwear at the National Art Library. It's a thesis, not a fetish.

For the rest of the six months, Fred will be living with his stepmother and his dad—Plan B and the Gazelle.

One of only two good things about us moving here is that I live closer to Fred now, which will be great when he gets back.

"Anyway," I said, hoping to reassure Posy, "who'd look after Howard if I topped myself?"

I was Howard's new meal ticket, and he wasn't letting me out of his sight. He looked up on cue when he heard his name—just one eye and one ear. Even in his preferred state of semiconsciousness, he knew exactly what was going down.

What the house smells of is piss, by the way. Soaked-in, marinated, wall-to-wall urine. We've been trying to get rid of it, but if you think spray-on deodorizer mixed with peed-on rugs is an improvement on the original smell, you're lucky you've never had to choose between them.

Howard is partly responsible, though definitely not to blame. He must have been stuck inside a lot. And by the time Adelaide died, she was using a bedpan at night. Fair enough, too—it would have been a major hike to the bathroom for a ninety-one-year-old. Also there were a few cats. The whole gang pretty much treated the house as one big toilet. The cats have scrammed.

Everything needs to be steam-cleaned. My mother is fighting with the Historic Homes Trust about who should pay. "They'll bloody own it all one day, why the hell shouldn't they cough up for freaking maintenance?"

"No freaking reason in the bloody world," I said. It really killed me when she used her polite mother swearwords.

She smiled at my amusement. "I'm a little overwrought."

"You can't tell."

That cheered her up a bit. Some people don't think sarcasm is funny, but we do, in our family. Our shrunken-up family. Our one-third-less-than-it-used-to-be family.

If you're wondering how my mother's coping with the whole gay-husband thing, she seems semi-okay. But it's hard to know for sure. Anytime I ask how she's feeling, she deflects with flippancy. "Spurned, but strong," she'll say, or "Bitter, but adjusting," "Hurt, but not vengeful"...

At least here I can't hear her crying at night.

I haven't heard anything from next door through the party wall, either, despite pressing my ear to every accessible section of it before remembering that the paint is probably original, lead-based, and therefore toxic. Possible lingering death added to my list of medium-term concerns.

The only noise I've heard is a kind of scratching and bumping from the attic sometimes.

I've investigated the noises and found certain unexpected things up there. When I found what I found, I had a choice. I may have made the wrong choice. Twice. And I'm still trying to figure out why I did what I did.

I've talked it over with Howard. I wish I knew what he thought. If I had to guess, I'd say it's a disapproval vibe. Hard to tell. I'm still at beginner-level dog, though he's clearly fluent in human. And I don't just mean English. He reads minds. It's unnerving.

My mother can be helpful when it comes to moral conundrums, but she's been missing in action lately, because of dealing with the breakup and trying to set up her business. That was another battle with the "bloody Historic Homes Trust."

She had to change the kitchen around a bit—get some shelves built, and have an industrial oven and fridge installed.

"And I hope we've seen the last of the rodents," she said. "Whatever you do, don't mention that if you happen to meet any customers, Dan."

"Even I know rats aren't a plus for a food business," I said, mildly offended.

"Please don't even say that word! I'm still traumatized."

She's going to be making wedding cakes. It wouldn't occur to everyone in the throes of a marriage breakdown, but we do irony in this house in addition to sarcasm.

5

I open the door to Fred—bespectacled, bepimpled, smiling Fred.

"My friend," I say.

A long pause.

"My friend," he responds.

It's so good to see him.

The long pause comes from a song my mother used to play in the car when she drove us home from school, "Rock and Roll Friend" by the Go-Betweens. There's a verrry long beat between two lines, and for no good reason, waiting for that second line used to really crack us up when we were little.

Then my mother would start laughing, too, and say,

"Have some respect. That's one of my favorite bands." It's a cold shock, remembering when she was really happy, versus now—brave smiles when she can manage them, grim when she thinks I'm not looking.

I stand back and let Fred in.

He hits the wall of smell.

"Man, that's bad. I thought you must have been exaggerating."

"It's worst for the first five minutes, then you start numbing out."

We pause in the hallway, coming into range of my mother on the phone. "What do you suggest I feed him on? He's a growing boy. And it still costs money, Rob, wherever he's at school."

Fred and I look at each other. I clear my throat. In front of anyone else that would have been really embarrassing.

"It doesn't stay this bad," he mutters. "The first few months are the worst." I steer us into the front sitting rooms. It's like a museum here. Like three huge houses' contents swallowed by one huge house.

With a sweeping gesture to the burdened mantelpiece, I say, "Objects d'art, Fred, feast your eyes."

"Yeah, thanks, 'cause the nose sure isn't. Feasting."

I draw back the faded velvet curtain, to throw some more light on the scene.

Fred takes a look around. "Holy moley. I've never seen this much . . . stuff."

I run through a few of the items.

20

"Japanned Regency armchairs with squab cushions—"

"Someone Japanned them? Since when is Japan a verb?"

"It's a lacquer finish. And squab—"

"What the cushions are stuffed with."

"Feathers of. There are no actual dead squabs in the cushions."

Fred punches me.

"I realize that, smart-arse."

There's nothing more satisfying than being stupid with a friend. Except an Estelle sighting. It feels weird there's a whole Estelle "thing" that Fred doesn't know about. I'm not ready to tell him yet.

"This is an English Pembroke table with perimeter decoration of inlaid boxwood. And this bulgy number is a boulle tea caddy," I say, remembering what Posy told me.

"What's fricken boulle?" Fred wants to know.

"Tortoiseshell with decorative brass inlay. Named after the guy who invented it."

"Right."

"And check this out." I take Fred over to the desk. "Rococo, ormolu mounts—that's gold-plated brass—and look underneath it…"

Fred gets on the floor and looks underneath the desk.

"It's not finished very well. It's really rough," he says.

"A telltale sign of authenticity. The reproductions are smoother underneath."

"What's it worth?"

"More than fifty grand."

I see Fred's fiendish mind cranking over.

"So we could sell this, substitute a copy, get fake IDs, plane tickets to LA, and fake drivers' licenses, and drive across America to New York, have ourselves a time, and be back in time for year ten. What do you say?"

"Yeah, one little flaw—we can't fake drive."

"We'd learn how in the wide-open spaces."

"Do you want to see my room?"

"Sure."

We head upstairs. Howard trots up after us.

My bedroom is on the top floor, at the back of the house. It has two sets of tall casement windows, with a tree right outside. While Fred canvasses Howard's range of tricks— sit and roll over—and gets to know him, I'm thinking if I were in a film, there would come a time when I'd swing out the window and climb down the tree. But this is life, and I'm not that keen to break my neck, so I use the stairs. And it's not as though my social life is so hectic I have to sneak out or anything. My mother would be relieved if I got asked out anywhere—she'd help me get there. She's consumed with guilt about me having to leave my school because of our financial crash. Because I'm smart and whatever. Extension this, acceleration that. You know the drill.

But in all the time I've spent hibernating in that creaking iron bed, buried under piles of old paisley eiderdowns whose faded colors have sopped up my sorry tears, I've realized this is my big chance to renovate the old image and keep it on the down low about being so smart. I can always do my accelerating in private, or just slow down for a bit. Cruise, coast, tread water—stop, preferably not sink...

Fred is snapping his fingers in my face.

"Come back, you've got the zombie look," he says.

"What?"

"I asked you how you're feeling about tomorrow."

"Like crap."

Fred nods. "I'm sorry I had to go away when I did. Have you spoken to your dad yet?"

I shake my head. "It's not because he's gay; it's because he's shot through and—upset Mum..."

Fred understands. "I know you're not some redneck homophobe, Dan."

"It's just so weird—my dad."

"I know."

"My dad is gay." I hear the disbelief in my own voice. It still hasn't properly sunk in, but it's a relief saying it out loud.

"I did a bit of research in London. It's more common than you'd think. The apparently heterosexual parent, you know."

There's no topic that Fred is squeamish about. He's a scientist. Always happy to apply the chloroform and start dissecting. This is still too raw for me, though, and I can tell he gets that. He's opening the door, but not barging in.

"Come around after school if you feel like it. I don't start till Tuesday. Plan B reckons I need a haircut."

"She's wrong," I say.

"I brought you back something. Don't hyperventilate; it's a British Museum pencil."

I smile, but now I'm starting to feel seriously sick about tomorrow. I know because of seeing her that first time in her uniform that Estelle goes to my new school. What if I'm in her class? What if I'm not? What's better: terror or disappointment?

6

It feels as though I'm thinking about Estelle most of the time. As though someone has changed my default setting to "Estelle" without my permission, or she's become my brain's screen saver. Desire has merged with a (completely alien) noble feeling of wanting to be able to offer Estelle my absolutely best self. The power of this is undercut by not really knowing what my best self is. But it's got to be more than the current sum of parts.

All this churning, and I haven't even met her. What's she going to think about me? Uncool me? Trying-to-hide-the-nerd me?

It's worse than just not being cool. I'm also going

through an awkward transitional stage. It's not that I'm ugly. I'm pretty sure I'm not. I'm tall and on the thin side. And I've grown a lot lately but haven't exactly filled out. I've asked my mother for protein powder, but you can imagine, what with the family budget and her short fuse these days, I didn't get a positive response. Then there's the fact that my girl experience is on the low side—or, more accurately, zero. I've never even kissed a girl. And I'm nearly fifteen.

My mother hands me a lunch bag, looks up—yeah, I'm taller than she is—and says, worried, "Just be yourself." Myself. My "self"? I don't really have a clue who that self is. It's like some kind of amorphous blob I'm trying to make into a better shape. I just know the bits I don't want to broadcast to a group of strangers.

1. Loser.
2. Nerd.
3. Gay dad.
4. Single mum, question mark over mental stability.
5. No cash.
6. Private-school refugee.

I don't want to be judged or pitied; I just want to stay under the radar while I look around.

At my old school, there was the usual assortment of jocks, try-hards, nerds, hard-cores, and cool groups. Then there were the odd socks, like me. Technically, I qualified for the nerds, but no way was I going to dock there.

Being left over is not a hugely bonding characteristic, so it's pure good luck that Fred and I turned out to be friends.

You probably think if I'm so smart, why did I even have to leave the school? Why wasn't I on a scholarship? I was, but it only paid for half the fees. My mother went to explain the family situation and see if they'd like to give me a full scholarship. They declined.

"Their loss," she said. But I could tell she was cut up about it.

The headmaster said they'd only be able to give a full scholarship to an "all-rounder." He may have been referring obliquely to my lack of athletic prowess. Also, private schools are big on you contributing to "school life," stuff like music and debating. And I don't talk that much at school.

>> <<

I'm here way too soon.

Walking in is grueling. I don't know a single person. I feel like a lemon rolling down the apple chute. I feel like turning around and going home.

But I brace myself. Not everyone gets a shot at the fresh start. I can be anyone I want to be. "Shy," "uncool," "nerd"—I can peel those labels off and flick them into the past. Who knows, maybe I'll fit right in. I can be an apple.

I hear someone yell out, "Dickhead. Hey, you. Dickhead."

I look around.

Why? Why would I do that?

There is an eruption of hysteria from the person who yelled out and his friends.

"Yeah, just checking it was you, dickhead."

They are amused. It's a good start to their day. There's hooting and back-slapping all around.

Don't react. Don't give them the satisfaction.

It could have been worse, I figure. Estelle could have seen it. And right on cue, as I turn and head for the main building, there she is, with two friends. No way they could have missed it.

So it's terror, not disappointment. Estelle is in my year-nine homeroom. So is the dickhead guy. His name is Jason Doyle, with the nauseating nickname "Jayzo."

The class has divided itself into legible groups: Jayzo and his crew, the alpha males; the cool group—creative interpretation of uniform, ignoring the new boy; some friendly-looking freaks who nod their welcome—lots of time spent on torturing hair, and piercings; a cluster of nerds talking about math; the blondes, in a teen-America time warp. Why hasn't anyone told them that's (no way) (omigod) (only) (like) (so) (totally) (random) (gay) and (way) (not) (cool) or (whatever)? I've tuned in. They use about twenty transposable words in all; quite efficient, I guess. The last pod is beautiful Estelle and her two beautiful friends floating above the rabble with their detached expressions and quiet, vital chat. And there are plenty of plasma kids—first impression: nondescript filler.

No matter how hard they try to be different, all the groups have one thing in common: each-otherness, something I'm conspicuously lacking in.

In the post-bell, pre-teacher squall, I watch Jayzo offering up an admittedly impressive wall of abdominal muscles to be punched. What a pitiful show-off. I think of my own flat but lacking-in-definition abs with a pang of gaping inadequacy. I have to do something about that.

"Nah, didn't feel it," he says to Dannii, one of the transposable parentheses girls. "Put your shoulder into it."

"No way." She giggles.

"Hard as you can. What are you scared of—breaking your hand?"

She does another pathetic little punch-and-giggle routine.

"You are, like, so totally buff!"

"Go on, harder." He notices me looking at them. "What are you looking at, faggot? Never seen a six-pack before?"

I turn away.

"Dickhead, I'm talking to you."

As if I'm going to fall for that one twice.

The homeroom teacher hurries in at this opportune moment. He scans the group, not looking at all sure that he recognizes any of them.

"We have a new student starting today. Are you here..." He consults a note. "Dan Cereal?"

Some snickers at the name.

"Cereill," I say. "It's pronounced 'surreal.'"

He touches his tongue to the trim under-edge of his moustache and sizes me up. Am I a troublemaker? Am I ridiculing him? He can't decide.

"If you prefer," he says. "Cereill it is."

Yes, I prefer my name pronounced properly. Call me crazy.

He nasal-drones his way through the roll. Estelle's friends are called Uyen Nguyen and Janie Bacon.

There's more to my social failures than not having kissed a girl and having no discernible abs. I don't even know any girls. And even way back in primary school when I did know some, I was never on their wavelength.

I was shy, and my mother used to tell me to "just join in." But that didn't work so well for me. It still embarrasses me, remembering some of my terminal clangers. One time in grade five I was sitting next to a girl I liked, psyching myself up to say something, anything, when *she* started speaking to *me*.

"There's this sky I really like," she whispered. We were

supposed to be drawing a map of national park areas in the Northern Territory.

"There's this sky I like, too," I said, *joining in*. "It's right after a storm, with the sun behind rain clouds, and the color is like dark gray trying to be purple."

"*Guy*. Not sky. He's a friend of yours."

"Oh. Who?"

But clearly the time for sharing was over.

"Just forget it."

She turned her back to me, pointing her knees out to the aisle. Neither of us could believe how stupid I was.

It's been pretty much all downhill from there.

And now my plan to avoid nerd and private-school refugee status is being dismantled by one careless comment from the teacher.

"Your academic record at Gresham is very impressive, Mr. Cereill. Let's hope your presence in math today provides some inspiration to us all."

Maybe, just maybe, if I say nothing at all in class, there's still a chance I can stay under the radar. I scowl and slouch lower in my chair. Someone behind me kicks the back of it so hard it rattles my spine.

The main differences between my old school and the new one are cosmetic. The old school was fat with generations of fees and bequests funding incessant improvements and maintenance, so the strains of music practice and umpires' whistles and plocking tennis balls were always accompanied by a background whine of power tools. This school has run-down buildings that look and smell like they don't get cleaned enough. There's not much space around it, and the oval is bald and muddy, fenced off with cyclone wire choked at the base with nettles and rubbish. They've given up on the graffiti front. And the bell is a loud, alarming siren that makes me feel like we're all about to be rounded up and shot.

I've successfully zoned out in math, so when the teacher asks me a question, I honestly don't know the answer.

Coming out of the classroom for lunch, Jayzo heaves his body sideways, slamming me into a bank of lockers in the same casual way jocks did that kind of thing at my old school. Prick.

Outside, I sit alone. A nerd-girl invites me to sit with her group, but I tell her I'm okay. I'm lying. I'm the opposite of okay. I'm nokay. I don't even have enough spit to swallow comfortably.

When any new kid started at my old school, he was given a year-level mentor, a prefect mentor, a house tutor mentor, and a teacher mentor, introduced around, signed up for extracurricular activities, forcefully integrated, then fully monitored. Here, it looks like I'm on my own. That means the image makeover will be difficult unless I talk to people. The only things anyone could possibly know about me are: tall, sometimes answers to "dickhead," silent in class, frowns, slouches, last name pronounced "surreal," not "cereal," chews with mouth shut.

Might be easier just to get *loser/loner* tattooed on my forehead and be done with it.

When school is over, I walk off through the screaming, shoving tangle of kids and go to Fred's. He's halfway between school and home. Plan B and the Gazelle both work at the university. Fred is the only kid from my old class who lives on this side of the city.

After a day of the impossible silent image makeover, which boiled down to me trying to look cool when I'm not, it's a relief to be heading toward Fred, who likes me well enough as I am.

When I get there, I walk right into the middle of Fred versus stepmother: the acne treatment showdown.

"It's not getting any better; I want the heavy artillery drugs," says Fred.

"You've got to at least give the cream a chance to work," says Plan B.

"Why can't we fast-forward? Cut to the chase?"

"We're doing exactly what the dermatologist recommends. It's not negotiable."

Fred changes tack.

"I'm pretty sure Mum agrees with me."

"Don't go there, Fred. Your mother, your dad, and I talk; you can't use wedge politics on us."

"That in itself is unfair. I'm the only kid I know from a broken home who can't win a trick."

"There's me now," I say. "I'm not winning any tricks."

"How's your mum's business going, Dan?" Plan B asks.

"Mostly trial cooking so far. But I think she's seeing her first client today."

"Smell fixed?" she asks.

"They were coming today."

"Temperature?"

"It's still a fridge." I'm playing for sympathy, and it works. She offers me a muffin.

"Say hi for me. And you..." She looks at Fred. "Take a coat and get a haircut while you're out."

"What time's the Gazelle home?"

"He'll be home by seven, and I wish you'd stop calling him that. He's trying to lose weight," she says.

≫≪

We walk past the shops on the way to my place.

Fred buys us Mars bars. He's fully briefed on my family's finances.

"Isn't this like pimples' favorite food?" I ask.

"Nah, that's crap. It's all about hormones and genes. I blame the Gazelle."

We walk along eating and checking out the shop windows.

At the Sacred Heart thrift store, I stop. Just what I need, sitting there, front and center—a big set of dumbbells.

They're five dollars, but when Fred tells the shopkeeper about me having no money, she lets us have them for a buck. Fred pays.

We're walking along carrying them—they're pretty heavy, ten pounds each—when I see Estelle coming toward us. It's too late for evasive action.

My heart is banging into my ribs. This will be our first actual face-to-face encounter. I want it to be perfect. I know there's not a hope in hell of that. She gives me a half-smile. Or maybe it's more of a semi eyebrow lift. Instead of eyebrow-lifting back, I stop and blurt: "These are not for me."

"Who are they for?" asks Fred, surprised.

"Well, they are for me, but I'm not using them as weights, I'm using them as..."

Fred catches on, better late than never, and comes to the rescue.

"Doorstops?"

"Yeah. Doorstops."

She smiles. "Oh, okay."

She says it very slowly, as though wondering why I'm telling her about them. I'm wondering the same thing.

She keeps walking.

"Bye, Estelle," I say to her back.

She turns. "How do you know my name?"

I freeze. Not only do I know her name, I also know she's named after her godmother, who lives in London. I know stuff I shouldn't know.

"We're in the same class," I manage to get out.

"Oh. Okay. Yeah," she says, and walks on.

"Who's she?" breathes Fred, through a stretch of fudge and caramel.

"She lives next door."

"She's hot."

As ever, master of the understatement.

"Raised as a heartbreaker?" He's referring to her near-namesake, Estella, in *Great Expectations* by Charles Dickens. We did it last year in Acceleration English.

"Knowing my luck, I'll never find out."

"Yeah, and thanks for introducing me," says Fred.

"She's my unattainable girl."

"All the more reason for introducing us. She's probably got unattainable friends who'd be perfect for me."

We walk on, weighed down literally and metaphorically.

7

When we get to my place, there's a big dirty silver tube sticking out of the front door, connected to a truck making a loud noise. Carpet Miracles are working their magic inside, and I walk into the house for the first time without feeling sick.

Fred sniffs like a terrier.

"That's an amazing improvement."

We walk deeper into the freezing gloom. Howard comes barking out to greet us, and my mother emerges from the back of the house with a young woman who looks as though she's been crying for quite a while.

"Thank you so much," she says, holding my mother's hand. "I could have ended up married to . . . my father."

In response to Fred's Jerry Springer–alert look, I say, "I think she's speaking about the personality type, not her actual father."

"Come back when you find the right Mr. Right," says my mother, who looks a bit teary, too.

The woman hiccups and sniffles her way out the front door.

"You can't run a wedding cake business if you talk them out of getting married," I say. My mother ignores this sound observation.

"How was school?"

Fred tries to take the heat. "I'm not back till tomorrow."

"Dan?"

"Meh."

Not satisfied with a "meh," she's about to launch into more annoyingly specific questions, so I cut her off at the pass.

"Is there anything to eat?"

"Sure. Wedding cake samples. Help yourselves. Only eat the old stuff in the end container. What are *they* for?" The dumbbells.

"Doorstops," says Fred. What a joker.

"Good, we need some more junk around here." She heads back to the kitchen.

Fred and I make our way along the checkerboard-tiled hallway, past enormous bookcases full of cracked leather-bound books, ancient orange and green Penguin paperbacks, and travel guides, and walls jammed with eighteenth-century engravings, wonky maps, and framed, fossilized lace and embroidered samplers. Fred pulls out a book, *The Chrysalids* by John Wyndham, and nearly drops it in surprise.

"That's awesome."

He shows me. A wasp has built its multipod cocoon along half the length of the book, the curly, delicate nest gluing the pages together like cement. The original inhabitants are long gone. A featherlight desiccated spider nestles in one of the little caves.

"You can keep it," I say.

"Don't the books belong to the trust, too?"

"They've taken away all the valuable ones. These are mostly pretty worthless, all filled with mildew or something."

We continue upstairs. The flowering carpet's dark colors remind me of a fairy tale book illustration from somewhere just outside the edge of my memory. Each step has a copper carpet rod. It must have been a pain for Carpet Miracles.

Fred stops for a good look. He's still getting his head around this joint. Even the upstairs landing is a kingdom of junk. He steps back, kicking into an elephant foot stand full of old umbrellas and walking sticks.

"It sucks that you can't sell some of this. You'd be set up."

"It's a very *water, water everywhere, nor any drop to drink* sort of bummer," I say.

"Very," he agrees.

That's from a poem we had to study where people are lost at sea, dying of thirst, as if you couldn't guess.

In my room, Howard prepares for a snooze. This involves him walking around in small circles, scraping and patting his bedding into shape. He's very fussy and doesn't relax until he's satisfied. Then he curls up, heaves an almighty sigh, and is snoring inside a second. I'm getting used to his sounds at night—it's like having a little engine sleeping next to you.

"When we got here, Howard ran upstairs and scratched like a maniac at the door of Adelaide's room. When we let him in, he went and got that and followed me to my room."

Howard cocks up one ear, as he always does when he hears his name.

"He remembered where his bed was? That's pretty good," says Fred.

"And I think it reminds him of Adelaide. It's a bunch of her old cardigans knotted together."

Howard snuffles down deeper, listening and agreeing.

"Who's that?" Fred asks, peering out the window.

There's a guy with luggage, letting himself into the building at the foot of the garden.

"Must be the stables guy. He gets to live out there for as long as he wants. Like us and the house."

"It'd be worth the trust's while to knock off him and your mum."

The same thought has occurred to me.

"I've told her to watch her back. She says it's the least of her worries."

"Which side's Estelle on?"

"Over there." I point to the left.

"So, you'd be able to hear her if she's in her garden."

"Yeah."

He looks up and around.

"You share a party wall with her," he says. "That's something you've got in common."

"Knockout icebreaker, Fred. I'll try that one."

"Where's your laptop?"

"School took it back. You know how they're leased..."

I can see Fred wants to kick himself. He hasn't had much time to adjust to my new no-money life.

"I was e-mailing you from our friendly municipal library when you were away."

"This is bad."

"Bad for me," I say, desperately trying to lighten it up for him. "Means I have to see you in person...actually talk to you."

"What about your phone?"

"Gone. But when I get a job, I'll get a prepaid."

"Where does that door go?"

"It's like a storeroom, airing cupboard, upstairs hot-water service, linen press sort of room."

Fred tries the handle. It doesn't open, because I've locked it, and the key is in my pocket.

"It's jammed," I lie. Howard snorts. Even in his semi-conscious state he's onto me. How does he do that?

Fred heads off to do his holiday homework, chomping on a piece of wedding cake sample—it's our only snack food—and I go back upstairs to feel bad all over again about my visit to the attic.

8

It happened about a week ago, when my mother was getting frantic about "rodents" and the impending council health inspection, which would mean she could, or could not, start operating her business.

We'd both been hearing the bumps in the night, and even though it sounded more like possums or cats than rats to me, I said I'd check it out. That night I dreamed of morose health inspectors, large rats in suits carrying clipboards, stepping around the happy little attic rats who'd come down to party in the kitchen, and I woke to a distinct scratching noise followed by a bump from overhead. It sounded like something being dropped, and it made the hair on the back of my neck stand up. I stuffed my head under a pillow but heard the scratching again. I sat up and dinted the pitch-darkness with my flashlight. Paper-sharp slices of wind were sighing through gaps in the window frames, moving the heavy curtains gently, so they looked to be breathing in and out. I shivered with cold and horror, and zipped the light around the room once more.

There was a dark shape near the door—it was Howard doing the scratching. I put on a sweater, grumbling but happy to take him out—better by a long shot than cleaning up something biological in the morning. And besides, I've promised him he'll never have to suffer the indignity of having to pee inside again.

As we walked along the landing, there was another distinct bump from overhead.

The next night after dinner, when my mother was elbow deep in marzipan research, I went into the storeroom and climbed the ladder attached to the wall under a trapdoor. Fourteen rungs. The old-fashioned rounded ones. They dug in, even through sneakers. The ladder was set out only a few inches from the wall. When I got to the top and undid the stiff trapdoor bolt, something was weighing down on the cover. It wouldn't budge. I gave it an awkward shove with my shoulder and head, and heard a crash from the other side as something heavy hit the attic floor.

I froze. Someone had tried to block this entrance to the attic. My mind cycled through a kaleidoscope of nasty possibilities—psychotic criminals, hungry rats, ghosts taking the form of small children with vacant eyes, sick little smiles, and pointy incisors...a vampire ghost? That's just dumb. Ghosts don't eat. It would have to be one or the other. Enough. I gave myself a mental smack on the side of the head, started breathing again, and ventured up another rung to take a look.

I zipped the flashlight beam around. Nothing scuttled or charged from the blackness, so I hauled myself into the space.

Like the rest of Adelaide's house, it was large, dusty, and full of stuff—mostly trunks and wooden storage crates. A box of books had been blocking the trapdoor cover and had tipped sideways and spilled when I shoved. Who had put it there? I walked around checking between trunks and bits of furniture. Whoever put the box there had either used another exit to get out of the attic, or they were still here. A wave of goose bumps shivered across my skin.

There must be another hatch down into the house. I found it hidden behind a huge camphorwood chest, but it, too, had a heavy box on top of it. Much as I searched around, I couldn't find a third access point back down into the house. It was creeping me out. I swung the flashlight beam up and looked into the roof cavity. There was the round window you could see from the street, but I couldn't imagine anyone getting out that way.

As the beam of light washed back down the party wall, I noticed a gap in the brickwork, about a door's width and half its height, blocked from the other side. This was the wall separating our attic space from Estelle's. Looking more closely, I could see the gap was blocked by flattened cardboard cartons. I gave a tentative push, and they fell in with a bit of a crash. I stopped breathing, but there was no response to the noise, so I crawled on through.

This was not a space for rats, or possums, or even ghosts. I saw in a glance that it belonged to a girl. I checked again, making sure I couldn't hear anything, and shone the flashlight around. My heart thumped like a maniac. Of course I knew I was trespassing, and not just by being on someone else's property—no, this was a private space. Despite that, there was no way I was leaving without looking around. I didn't consciously decide to stay and snoop; I just did it.

There were candles everywhere—in a huge pair of blackened silver candelabras sitting in the middle of the floor, in tall crystal candlesticks, in small Venetian glasses. There was a large nest made up of brocade curtains, faded cushions, and intricately patterned patchwork quilts. Next to it was a pile of books and a mohair rug.

On a small desk sat: a glass paperweight; a miniature black lacquer Chinese cabinet with hand-painted ivory inlay panels—I can't help the cataloging, it's all that time I spent with Posy; some very old journals filled with delicate copperplate writing; a doll with a porcelain face, dressed in French sailor clothes; some notebooks and pens; a small bottle carved from pale green jade. Embroidered silk shawls decorated the walls. Estelle had tied ribbon loops onto the corners of the shawls and pinned them up with drawing pins. Overlapping Persian rugs half covered the unpolished boards. Some of the candles must have been scented, because the place smelled like vanilla, and something spicy.

I opened a few of the cabinet drawers—a stash of sweets, some beads, a few little silk tassels, some pens, and three dead Christmas beetles.

The sound of a door shutting loudly made me flick off the flashlight and listen as though I were one giant ear.

It was Estelle, singing loudly, the way people do when they're attached to an iPod. She had a good voice.

Then I heard someone else, although Estelle obviously didn't.

"Estelle, Estelle! *Estelle!*" Knock, knock, knock. *Knock knock knock.*

That must have penetrated because Estelle said, "What?"

" 'Yes, Mum,' " the person corrected.

"Yes, Mum, what is it?"

"There's a good documentary on in a few minutes on early Renaissance art."

"Pass."

"I wish you'd speak in sentences."

"I'm not interested in the documentary."

"How do you know unless you come down and look at it?"

"Instinct."

She must have put her earbuds in again, because her mother turned up the volume to say, *"How can you study with that thing on?"*

"I'm not studying. It's holidays..."

Then her mother must have left, shutting the door after her.

"...you cow," Estelle added.

"I heard that."

"Give the woman the geriatric audiology medal," Estelle said.

"I heard that, too," her mother said, from the other side of the door.

"Well, if you'd just go *away*, you wouldn't hear anything!"

"If you keep listening to that thing at high volume, you won't hear anything by the time you get to my age."

"I don't give a shit."

"Right! You're grounded! You do not use language like that to me!"

"I didn't know you were still there. Why are you still there?"

"To remind you that you *should* be doing homework. I don't know why I'm spending money on those Alliance classes otherwise."

"So, stop. It's not like I asked to do them."

Her mother obviously gave up and left.

There was enough streetlight seeping in through the round window to allow me to creep out without tripping over anything. But then there was the problem of the packing boxes. They'd been easy enough to push through, but how was I going to manage the reverse maneuver? I stacked them together and leaned them against the wall. I crawled through to my side of the attic and tried to slide the boxes back over the gap, but it wasn't possible from this side. I needed...string. I switched the flashlight on and started searching. I found a long piece of cord attached to a folded curtain. I ripped it off and took it back to the gap. Climbing through again, I looped the cord around the boxes. Then when I backed through the gap I could pull and jostle them into the right position, and carefully pull the cord away from the boxes and back through to my side. I listened—nothing fell. I rolled the cord up and left it on the floor for next time.

It probably should have worried me that I was planning so coolly to trespass again, to spy. How did that mesh with wanting to be good? Not at all, apparently. Stick it on the list to worry about later.

I noticed a tiny cardboard box on the floor next to the wall. There had been a couple in Estelle's attic, too. I picked it up: POISON. KEEP OUT OF REACH OF CHILDREN AND ANIMALS. PEST CONTROL IS OUR BUSINESS. RODENT POISON. DO NOT HANDLE.

Estelle's parents must have had the eradicators in. I went downstairs and reported a clean bill of health for the attic.

There was another visit to the attic. But that's the one I can't talk about.

9

With Fred gone, I'm back downstairs, still hungry and rummaging for more food. I know it's to do with growing so much, but there's not a single time of day I couldn't happily scarf down a couple of burgers or meat pies, if they happened to be handy.

"There's nothing to eat!"

"There's bread. And fruit."

"We haven't even got any good fruit. Those apples are ready for the compost," I mutter in a hunger-induced grump. "And there aren't any chocolate cookies, or muffins, or potato chips, or Shapes."

"They're luxuries now, I'm afraid."

"We don't even have good leftovers anymore!" I close the fridge door very firmly.

"Because we eat what we buy now, and there's certainly no fat in the budget to throw good food into the compost."

She's getting angry now, or upset, so I back off before it develops.

Our life has come to this. We're stuck on the essentials iceberg, watching all the good stuff float past on the luxury iceberg. They used to be joined.

When she suggests we make muesli bars, I agree with feigned enthusiasm and genuine hunger. It's not too hard. You mix oats, sugar, flour, and coconut with some melted butter and honey—we use golden syrup, because it's cheaper—press the mixture into a pan, and bake it.

"Your dad called."

I don't respond.

"I understand how you must be feeling, but at least he's making an effort to stay in touch. Other fathers would have given up long ago, faced with the wall of silence."

How can she understand how I'm feeling? I certainly don't. But I can't be bothered asking for enlightenment— it would just mean more talking. Shared adversity is supposed to be a bonding experience, but it's not kicking in for us yet.

"If he wanted to see me so much, he could have moved into this dump with us."

She puts her arm around my shoulder and gives a

squeeze. I lift my elbow out so she can't get too close. "He's trying."

"It's his fault you've got to do all this," I say, looking around the kitchen—the catering-size containers of flour and dried fruit, the extra-wide oven, the range of cake tins that will eventually produce those tiered, multilevel-edifice wedding cakes.

"I don't mind. I'm a very good cook. I've found a premium-priced, high-profit-margin niche item to specialize in. I have experience in marketing. The bank has enough faith in me to give me a start-up loan. It's all under control."

You can hear how relaxed she sounds.

She's still running on the postseparation adrenaline surge. Reality hasn't quite hit. Unfortunately, there's only me to lend a hand when it does. I've Googled this. She needs to express her anger so it doesn't lead to posttraumatic stress disorder, manifesting itself in anxiety, depression, and ultimately, substance abuse.

She watches as I plow through half the batch of muesli bars.

"You need to express your anger," I say.

"Where would that get us?" she asks, smiling for some reason.

I don't want to go into the whole substance-abuse risk scenario, in case it makes things worse, so I change the subject.

"What's for dinner?"

"Vegetable and chickpea curry with rice."

I groan, on the inside. She makes this by the vat. It's nutritious, satisfying, and cheap. That's the official word. But I'm sick of the sight, smell, and taste of it. Pasta alla nothing-much-on-it and soup with a lot of bread are the other new staples. Juicy steaks, big roasts with lots left over for sandwiches, and once-a-week takeout are fuzzy-edged memories.

She fixes her X-ray eyes on me and pounces just as I've settled into a nostalgic scan of my favorite takeout foods.

1. Margherita pizza.
2. Meatball sub.
3. Nachos. Hold the sour cream.
4. Hamburger with the works. Hold the beetroot.
5. Pad Thai noodles and chicken satay.
6. Fish and chips

"So how was school, really?"

Fish and chips catches me unawares, my throat jams with a lump of solid tears, remembering the smell of vinegar, ripping into the burning paper parcel, the cypress pines along the edge of the park, the pier, my dad...how many times have we done that?

"Fine."

"Talked to anyone yet?"

"No."

"You will make friends, Dan."

"Is that an order?"

She chooses to ignore my rudeness. "It's hard for people to get to know you unless you speak."

"I was planning to transmit messages using only the power of my brain waves. I guess I'll have to rethink that," I say. That's pissy, but it comes out before I have time to edit.

She gives me the compressed-lips, narrowed-eyes *you're being difficult, but I'm saving my anger for the big issues* look.

I'm spared the next onslaught by a knock at the back door. It's the stables guy. He looks like he's in his late twenties, about ten years younger than my mother. He's got a slight cockney accent—sounds like it dates back quite a while, but he's kept it cooking along because he thinks it sounds cool. A wanker for sure.

As they go through their introductions—he's called Oliver—he admires what my mother's done with the kitchen.

"I wouldn't have recognized it, Julie. I can see great things happening here."

What is he? A mystic or something? The wedding-cake psychic?

They yap on about Adelaide. And he's showing no sign of leaving.

"So, it's just the two of you here?" he asks.

What's it to him? Is he planning to rent out the empty bedrooms?

My mother nods. "Rob and I separated recently."

Oh, no, personal overdisclosing.

Uncomfortable pause.

"I hope you don't mind me being out there," Oliver says. "I feel like a bit of an interloper."

You got that right, buddy.

"Not at all. Please don't think that for a minute. Adelaide adored Lettie. And she was terribly fond of you."

"It was mutual. She was an amazing woman."

Now I'm going to puke.

Oliver looks at me. "Lettie was my grandmother."

"Right," I say. Like I care. What is he still doing here? Trying to hit on my mum? Get an accommodations upgrade from the stables to the big house?

I try to figure out what sort of work he does based on his clothes. He's wearing jeans, a funny blue-black color, a bean-green sweater with very long sleeves that halfway cover the backs of his hands, and black riding boots with red elastic. Straight blond hair parted on the side, dull metal framed glasses... It's a toss-up between filmmaking and architecture.

"What do you do?" I ask.

"I'm a trend analyst and forecaster," he says.

"Which is what exactly?"

"Dan." It's the *rude tone of voice* category reprimand, but I can tell Oliver is way too sure of himself to be offended.

"I plant myself in a city, spend time on the streets and in clubs and bars watching and talking to people to check out what they're wearing, eating, drinking, talking about, and listening to, what toys and gadgets they're playing with. Then I make some recordings, take some pictures, shoot some footage—write it all up, show advertising agencies and their clients, and by the time I've done the presentations I'm ready to go away and take a look somewhere else. So I basically help advertisers chase their tails."

"What a fun job," my mother says.

It does sound good, but this guy's impressed enough with himself without me joining the fan club.

"I'm taking the dog for a walk," I say.

Howard stands stiffly and walks slowly to the back door. He looks a bit...annoyed. Tail down. Aren't dogs supposed to be up for a walk anytime, night or day?

"Look, he must know what *walk* means," my mother says.

"Not a lot Howard doesn't know," says Oliver, patting him on the way through.

Howard's tail goes up. He shakes his head and stands tall—as tall as a little dog can, anyway.

My motive in taking Howard out is mixed. I'm also hoping to run into Estelle. A marrow-chilling half hour later, there is still no sign of her. Strange the way you can feel relieved and devastated at the same time. I head for the shopping strip—I have to try to get a job. The shops are mostly cafés and specialty food stores, homemade pasta, an organic grocery, a few clothes shops, and an art gallery. Then there's the thrift store, a hardware store, and a news agency. A tram squeals around the corner as I tie Howard to the leg of a bench and steel myself to approach the thrift store for work. I can't believe my luck when they hire me on the spot—Tuesday and Thursday after school. Easy!

I'm heading home when people start spilling out of a tall doorway between two shops. They look about my age, chatting away to one another. I notice they're disabled, mostly Down syndrome, I think. And Estelle comes out behind them, walking with a girl, holding her hand.

Estelle's smile is a mile wide. She has light brown hair that's dead straight, parted in the middle, and tucked behind her ears. Her hair gleams; she must wash it every day. Her ears are neat and pretty. Her eyes are dark blue or gray. I haven't had a long enough look yet to tell.

When she sees me, the smile amps down a bit—no mistaking it—but she can't avoid me. I've walked into the group, and these kids are milling around, joking with one another, saying their good-byes—they've got all day. Estelle is trapped. It's probably the only reason she says hi.

"Who are you?" asks the girl she's with.

"Phyllis, this is ... I'm sorry, is it Dan?"

"Dan it is," I answer. Dan it is? What do I sound like? A leprechaun? This is bad.

"He's moved in next door," explains Estelle, probably hoping to make it quite clear to Phyllis that that is the only reason she's speaking to me.

"Adelaide's house?" Phyllis checks.

"That's the one," I say. Again, with the language. Couldn't I have said "Yeah"? Now I sound like a game show host.

"She died in her bed," says Phyllis.

"Yeah." *Now* I pull a "yeah" in entirely the wrong place. I sound heartless, the sort of guy who couldn't care less where some old lady dies.

I'm desperate to prolong and preferably improve the quality of my time with Estelle, so I volunteer a bit of information, which is not an easy thing for me to do. "I just got a job."

"Where?" she asks.

"The thrift store."

"Volunteer work," says Phyllis. "You're nice to help out."

The obvious had escaped me. Not for the first time. Of course the thrift store doesn't pay people—it's a charity shop. For someone supposedly smart, I am the prize idiot of all time. I feel my face going red and blotchy with foolishness and hope it might pass for the effect of the cold wind.

"Yes, I think it's just really important to make an, er... contribution. I'm looking for paid work, too, if you hear about any."

"We'll let you know," says Estelle. She's about to walk on, and I make a second herculean effort to keep her with me.

"Where were you coming out of?" This is killing me;

I sound like English is my second, or possibly third, language.

"It's a studio program," says Phyllis. "Artists work with us, up there." She's pointing to the second floor, above the shops. Then anticipating my next question: "They don't need anyone."

"Except me," says Estelle. "But that's volunteering, too."

"Did you two meet there?"

They laugh.

"No. Primary school," says Estelle.

"Do you know what happened to Adelaide's dog?" asks Phyllis.

That hits me over the head like a gigantic cartoon frying pan, with a ringing clunk.

Howard! I've completely forgotten about him. He's still tied to the bench across the street—if I'm lucky. If he hasn't already been picked up by the local animal shelter, or dognapped.

"He sort of comes with the house. Only, I've left him over there . . . Gotta run," I burble, taking off, almost colliding with a cyclist, who spews a stream of vivid abuse in my trail.

It is such a relief to see old Howard, patiently sitting there. He gives a sharp bark as I untie him.

"I know, I know. Dog ownership for dummies: Take dog out; bring dog home."

Usually it's the human who trains the dog. But when

Howard wags his tail, I'm the one responding to the approval and remembering for next time.

Estelle and Phyllis are heading off, and I've missed my chance to walk with them. Although, with my level of smooth moves, I don't know how I would have managed the three abreast, plus dog on leash, walk and talk without tripping over someone, probably myself.

Howard and I mooch on home, checking all the windows for real jobs. The only one is in a clothes shop and says RETAIL EXPERIENCE ESSENTIAL. Mrs. Nelson at the thrift store waves as we walk past. I wave back, feeling like a complete knob.

By the time we get home, my mother and Oliver are looking pretty damn chummy, with an almost finished bottle of wine on the table. He must have supplied it, seeing as wine is a luxury. From the way he looks at me— sympathetic, understanding (why does everyone think they understand?)—I can tell she's blabbed the full family catastrophe. What is the woman on? We don't even know this guy. After years of warning me about it, has the whole stranger-danger concept suddenly escaped her? Do I have to do all the worrying around here? Yes and yes, apparently. And what happened to the notion of privacy? Stuff that's my business, stuff that I might not want to share with the whole world? Out the window.

I can't believe my ears when she invites him to stay for

dinner. Thankfully, he's got other plans. What would Dad think? Well, of course, he wouldn't care. If he did, he'd be here, going through all this crap with us. Instead of... I don't know what he's going through by himself, but it's his choice. So screw you, Dad. I hope you feel as bad as I do. But still somehow I feel a whole lot worse thinking of him by himself.

I try to escape straight after dinner, but no such luck.

"Dan, you're not going anywhere; I need your help," says my mother. I stay, but she's fuming now because I said "whatever." She hates that word. Her rant goes on in the background while we give the kitchen an almighty scrub down and I wonder about my dad. How *is* he doing? Where's he staying? Is he hungry like me, now that there's no money? How often does he think about us? Should I talk to him when he calls? How long will he keep trying before he gives up on me? Before he drifts off, another ice berg that used to feel so securely attached?

"Dan, watch what you're doing! You're flooding the place."

An exaggeration. I tipped one bucket of water over the floor. The way they wash down decks, in movies. How else do you wash it? Since I was little we've had a procession of nice Mrs. Somebodies doing all our dirty work around the house, so it's not as though I've participated in this sort of thing before. Does she think it's instinct? Are babies born knowing this stuff? Is it contained in our DNA? I doubt it.

"*Dan!*"

Uh-oh. More water down. I'm not concentrating.

"Leave me to finish this. You're no help at all," says my mother, red in the face with anger and effort. She's not used to this cleaning caper, either.

"And tomorrow, I'm going to show you how to clean a bathroom."

I can't wait.

Inventory of can'ts:

1. Can't wash floors.
2. Can't talk to girls, especially Estelle.
3. Can't get a job that pays.
4. Can't look after Howard when I take him out.
5. Can't trust the stables guy.
6. Can't talk to my dad.

There are more. Let's be frank. This list could run to thousands.

10

Over breakfast—cereal and four pieces of toast with peanut butter and jam—I try to warn my mother about getting too friendly with Oliver, but she's not buying it.

"You're being silly. He's perfectly pleasant."

"That's how they lure people in. The best psychopaths are the plausible ones. Everyone knows that."

"He seems well adjusted; he's employed; he has a sense of humor; he has a girlfriend."

"I'll believe that when I see it."

"She's in London."

"London, or feeding fish in the Yarra? And how do we know Adelaide didn't come to a sticky end, for that matter?"

"Dan, she was ninety-one. All her money's gone to the gallery. And Oliver wasn't even here when she died. He was in New York."

"The smart ones always have watertight alibis."

My father would have handled this better. I didn't mean to end up in the middle of a murder mystery. I just don't want my mother going all instant-best-friends with the guy.

"All I'm saying is we don't really know him."

"Adelaide virtually grew up with his grandmother *and* knew his parents, and he's part of our life now, for as long as we're here, so it makes sense that we get to know him."

"That doesn't mean you have to tell him everything."

"I decide what I will or won't tell people. And you can decide what you tell people."

We never used to argue all the time like this.

The phone rings. My mother nods at me to answer it. But she's got this brilliant idea now that we have to answer the phone saying the business name, so I shake my head and take another huge bite of my toast, chewing defiantly. She spits her mouthful into her hand and answers in a calm way, belying the murderous look on her face. "*I Do Wedding Cakes*, how may I help you?" It's a wrong number. We sit there glaring at each other.

Walking to school, I wonder how long I can avoid answering the phone. I decide it's got to be for as long as she's running the stupid business. And seeing as how our live-lihood depends on the business being a success, it looks like I'll never answer the phone again. Just as well no one's calling me.

First period is science. They—we—are doing a biology unit.

I'm looking into the dish trying to take deep, even breaths. We're inspecting raw eggs. The teacher, Ms. Peale, is enthusing. "See the stretchy chainlike substance between the yolk and the white? It's called the chalaza." She writes the word on the whiteboard. "There are two in each egg; they anchor the yolk in the thick egg white. Some of you may be lucky enough to see brownish lumps of protein in your yolks; that's undeveloped embryonic matter."

I'm feeling the familiar swooning dizziness that happens just before I faint. Don't let it happen in front of Estelle. Please. Get ahold of yourself. Resist. Avoid public humili-ation. Breathe.

Ms. Peale presses on. "Put your fingers into the egg white. Feel that slidey, albuminous viscosity. And note the yolk's tough outer membrane; it's called the vitelline mem-brane. Touch it. Feel that bouncy resistance. In a fertile egg, the luscious yolk will nourish the growing embryo." I try to put my mind anywhere other than this slimy puddle of goop.

Jayzo and friends help. I concentrate on their idiotic asides, and the swoony feeling fades a bit. Forgetting that *the* guiding principle of underage sex is avoiding pregnancy, they are offering to fertilize the eggs of Dannii and the transposable parentheses. Like I'm the expert. But at least I've got some basic theory up my sleeve.

I see Estelle look at them in disbelief. I try to catch her eye to share a disbelief moment, but her glance skates across me as though I'm not here.

Then Ms. Peale gets me from left field. "By the way, *yolk* is also the word for the greasy secretions exuded by sheep's skin to keep the wool soft."

I'm really struggling to keep it together, when I see Jayzo's friend Deeks swallow his raw egg, nearly gag, then grin triumphantly. He's won ten bucks.

I crash.

Ms. Peale's worried face is the first thing I see when I open my eyes. For one weird and scary beat, I have absolutely no idea where I am. It comes back to me like waking into a bad dream. Ms. Peale and a girl called Lou are helping me get into a chair and keep my head down.

Between flicking bits of raw egg around, and hanging it on me, Jayzo and crew are probably having their best-ever science lesson. "You're a dickhead, Cereal," Jayzo says.

"It's Cereill," I manage.

"Cyril, next time you're feeling faint, please sit down with your head between your knees or go out for some fresh air, okay?" Ms. Peale says.

"It's Dan, not Cyril."

"Have you fainted before, Dan?"

"Yes. It's not a big deal."

"No big deal for Cereill to act like a girl," says Jayzo, in a labored attempt at humor that has his friends rolling in the aisles.

"You're a real wit, Jayzo. The seven-letter variety," says Lou. She smiles at me sympathetically. I glance over to Jayzo to see how he's handling the stinger she's thrown his way. He looks blank.

"Don't worry," says Lou. "He can't count and he can't spell."

Lou breaks away from some plasma companions to sit with me at lunchtime. She reminds me of Fred, and it's not just the glasses and pimples. She gives me the lowdown on some of the people sitting near us.

"First girl to put out at a party. Can get drugs from her older brother. Hooked up with five girls on New Year's Eve and they all got mono. Mean and stupid and a jock. (Jayzo.) Not mean, but unapproachable, keep to themselves. (Estelle and her friends.) Parents are heroin addicts. Medicated for ADHD. Parents are political advisers. Smart, but plays dumb. Frequent flyer at the children's court. Nice, but uncool. Stabbed a kid with a compass in grade five. Older sister had an affair with the math teacher, who got fired..."

"What about you?" I ask Lou.

"Smart, not mean, not popular, problem skin, will

67

emerge like a butterfly one day and pretend not to recognize Jayzo and his moronic compadres when they carry my groceries to my smart but fuel-efficient European sports car." She smiles. "I'll probably still be a caterpillar, but I should be able to sort out the pimples."

"What about me?"

"I don't know yet...Doesn't say much, faints, new..."

"Already unpopular."

"Only because of Pittney blabbing about your academic record and your private school. That's more than enough reasons for you to be despised by them..." She nods in Jayzo's direction. "How come you changed schools?"

"Expelled. Playground violence. Rampant drug use."

She laughs. "No, why really?"

"We're—broke." And broken.

"And what's with the eggs and fainting?"

"It happens sometimes with stuff that's slimy, raw, or just disgusting. I guess I'm a bit phobic. I start feeling hot and sick, and then...you saw what comes next."

"I don't have any phobias, personally, but my favorites are arachibutyrophobia, which is..."

"Fear of peanut butter sticking to the roof of your mouth."

"Very good. And I like triskaidekaphobia, too. Fear of the number thirteen."

"My favorite is luposlipaphobia."

"Which is...?"

"Fear of being chased by timber wolves around a kitchen table while wearing socks on a newly waxed floor."

She laughs. "Sure it is."

"Okay, it's a *Far Side* cartoon," I admit. "But it's still my favorite."

We look at each other with shy relief. It's the look two odd socks give when they recognize each other in the wild.

11

Three shifts in at the thrift store, and it feels like a lifetime. Or a life sentence. How could I be so stupid as to sign on thinking it was a paying gig? Mrs. Nelson being one of the nicest people on the planet just makes it worse.

I don't think she needs the extra hands, either. But I can't talk to her about it. I don't want to seem like a quitter. Volunteering today, it's me, three women, and a guy on a community service court order. Six of us. It's too crowded behind the counter, so Mrs. Nelson gets me to tidy up some shelves. I slightly overload one, and it crashes. Lucky for me, only a couple of things get broken. Plus tidying up the mess gives us all something to do. We've had one customer in the last forty-five minutes.

I've just wished for the hundredth time for more customers so time will stop dragging, when Jayzo, Deeks, and Dannii arrive, all slurping slurpies from the service station. How can they when it's so cold?

"Hey, look, it's Cereal," Jayzo says, sauntering in.

"Cereill."

"What are you doing in the povvo shop, Cereal?"

"I work here."

He nods insolently at Mrs. Nelson. "Aren't you going to introduce us to your mum?"

"She's not my mother," I say, in a tone of such firm denial I realize it must sound insulting.

"Sorry, pal, your girlfriend, then."

Deeks and Dannii snicker.

I go bright red and try to ignore them.

Mrs. Nelson steps up and asks if she can help them with anything.

"No way," says Dannii, with a long slurp. "We're totally, like, just looking."

The three of them ask the price of half the contents of the shop. The community service guy is sweating, and the old ladies are tutting and frowning.

As they are leaving, Jayzo "accidentally" spills what's left of his slurpy into the bin of one-dollar books—some of our biggest movers. I apologize and try to clean it up, feeling obliged to look agreeable when the old ladies go on and on about the young people of today and speculate that they were probably on ice. The community service guy and I share a smile over that one. They were just on sugar and terminally low brain-wattage.

Then I have a talk with Mrs. Nelson, who wants the names of "those young bullies" so she can call the school. I manage to convince her that they're just "troubled," and ask if I can leave ten minutes early. Mrs. Nelson seems almost relieved.

My mother is at the front door when I get home, looking more than usually pleased to see me. Before I can get inside, she's shoving a pile of Howard's food, bowls, and toys into my arms, handing me Howard, on his leash, and telling us to scram. She can't remember if dogs are allowed to live on premises where food is being prepared for sale, and doesn't have time to check the regulations before the inspectors are due to arrive.

"Where should I take him?"

"I don't know. Just disappear for an hour." I stand there, not sure where to go.

"Move it, Dan. They're due now," she says, giving me an encouraging little shove.

She could at least be polite when banishing her only child.

There's too much stuff to lug along for a walk in the park. Fred's place is a good ten minutes away. That leaves Estelle—certain embarrassment—or Oliver the stables guy—possible murder or kidnapping.

>> <<

Estelle looks at me, Howard, and all the stuff, clearly astounded to see us at her door.

"If you're running away from home, you probably need to run a bit farther," she says with an encouraging smile, going to close the door.

"It's my mother—I mean, it's Howard."

She leaves the door open just a crack.

"If you're looking for a foster family for Howard, it's not us. Sorry. We're just not that nice. And everyone around here knows he pees inside." She shuts the door firmly, or maybe it's the wind.

I walk down half a block and turn right at the house with the bikes and Tibetan prayer flags on the veranda, into a bluestone lane, then right again, and I'm in the alley that backs on to our house. I keep walking and stop outside the back door of the stables building. There's music coming from inside. The Pixies, "Motorway to Roswell." My dad had that CD. Where did all his music go? We don't have it. Did my dad take it? Did the liquidators get it?

I guess this means stable guy is home. Should I risk it? Then it occurs to me that I don't need to. No reason I can't just sit down here and wait for an hour. Problem solved.

If it weren't so cold, I'd be perfectly comfortable leaning here against our bright blue recycling bin. I can smell Howard's chewie sticks; they smell deliciously like bacon.

He's still living the high life on the supplies Adelaide had stockpiled. I wonder if humans can eat the dog chews. If they smell this good, how bad can they taste?

A high-tech electronic click and buzz sound, and a gate swings open a bit farther down the alley. Estelle emerges with an armful of newspapers.

She almost jumps out of her boots at the sight of me sitting here between our respective recycling bins. Maybe it looks as though I'm about to eat a dog chew. What's the right thing to say in this social situation?

I go for "Hi."

"What the hell...? What are you doing here? Have you locked yourself out?"

At that moment, I hear my mother's voice. She's talking to the council inspectors.

"Bins never come through the house; they're collected from the alley," she says.

Her voice is getting closer. "I'll bring the bins in now, and you can see for yourselves. I keep them just over here."

"That's your mum, isn't it? So you can go in the back gate," Estelle says.

I shake my head furiously. There's too much to explain, no time to do it, and I can't manage to get a word out.

"What's wrong?" Estelle asks, perplexed. "Have you been kicked out?" She looks at the dog food. "Are you hungry?"

Howard starts barking and whining, as though he's worried. Join the club.

Instead of giving Estelle a rational answer, I shake my head again, and wave my free hand back and forth in front of my face in a demented *shut up* or *I can't talk* signal attempt, as our old gate is being jiggled and unbolted right behind my back.

Estelle is increasingly bewildered as I gather Howard and all his paraphernalia, scramble to my feet, and run off down the alley as fast as I can manage, just as the gate creaks and swings open.

Howard, excited by the sudden activity, barks his head off as we run. I don't dare look back. When I reach the end of the alley, I duck, panting, into the first open gateway. It's the yard area of the corner shop. The fence that backs onto the alley is covered with jasmine that is either holding it up or pushing it over. Inside the yard are stacks of empty pallets and crates, bins, and an outside toilet. A black cat and two tabbies take half-hearted swipes at one another in a puddle of winter sun. I grip Howard's leash. He's barking and the cats are meowing, but his tail is wagging like mad. He must not have the cat-aggression gene.

Howard breaks free as a woman comes out from the back of the shop. He jumps all over her, tail in propeller mode. She rubs his ears in exactly the way he loves.

"And who's your friend, Howard?" she asks him, smiling at me. "Are you the nephew, young man?"

"I'm Dan. I think it's great-nephew, or something."

"Good to meet you, Dan. I'm Mary Da Silva. Wait right here," she says.

She comes back out a minute or two later and hands me a lumpy paper bag.

I notice the humungous diamond earrings she's wearing. She's the one who got the rocks. They look kind of awful but great with her bright pink sari and red fleece hoodie.

"Bones," she says, nodding at the bag. "Give him one once or twice a week. Good for his teeth. I used to feed the gang each night when I brought Adelaide's dinner. These three moved in here when home delivery stopped. You can take them back, if you want."

I shake my head. "My mother's allergic. And she's running a food business. We don't even know if we're allowed to have Howard." I realize I'm blabbing private stuff and for all I know her husband is the council health inspector. "But please don't mention that to anyone. I couldn't stand it if we had to get rid of him."

She taps the side of her nose. "I'm a tomb, Dan. Is that the correct idiom? Or do I mean a grave?"

"Like, 'your secret will go with me to the grave'?"

"Just so!"

"Thanks for that."

"Your mother never stopped coming by to visit, but Adelaide wouldn't see her toward the end. I tried to get cleaners in, too, but all to no avail. She said she'd seen enough people, and done enough talking."

Howard is looking up at her with his tail down, as though he understands what she's saying.

"You don't need anyone to work in your shop, do you?"

"No. You could try Phrenology, though. Speak to Ali, the tall bald man. He uses part-time staff."

I get into a bit of trouble at home for lurking too close to the inspection zone, but it's not severe. My mother's got the official green light for the kitchen to operate commercially. You would think she'd be happy, but after dinner she's just sitting with the missing-in-action face listening to Radiohead, so I leave her communing with her sadness and her favorite band, and go upstairs for my first weight-training session.

Lying flat on my back, my arms stretched out in a *T*, I can see two things that make me uncomfortable. The first is dust balls that have been mating in captivity under my bed. Nestled in the herd's midst is an unopened present from my dad.

It seems that getting used to my dad being gay would be a lot easier if he'd bothered hanging around so I could talk to him about it. But I straightaway know that's not exactly fair. He's been calling me since he left. So technically, it's me not being available to talk.

Howard is the only one I can discuss it with. I'm beginning to think that getting used to my dad being gay is something like going into the ocean. It's freezing to an unbearable level for a while, then once you're in, it feels fine and you wonder what the problem was. Unfortunately, I'm still only in up to my ankles, taking chickenshit steps.

Lifting the two weights is a gut-straining debacle. As much as I heave, I can barely get them off the floor. Lifting one, with both hands, at chest level is more manageable.

The second thing I cannot avoid seeing as I lie here is the ceiling. Straight through that ceiling is the attic, and next to that attic is Estelle's attic.

I'm obsessing about Estelle. It's killing me knowing how much we have in common but being unable to convey this burning fact due to severe social disability. (*How* I know we have so much in common is in a category of worry I can't even discuss with Howard.)

When I think about the gaffes-to-date list, it seems unlikely I'll ever be friends with Estelle, let alone have anything resembling a romance with her.

Estelle has seen me:

1. Answer to "dickhead"—whale of a first impression.
2. Forget to bring Howard home.
3. Fail to answer a simple math question.
4. Nearly vomit in class.
5. Faint in class.
6. Act like a prize idiot in the alley.

Could I be making a worse impression?

When is the tide going to turn?

In my churning inadequacy, I lose count of the reps and accidentally let the weight crash into my face.

12

My mother obviously doesn't hear my agonized moaning over Radiohead's agonized moaning or I'm sure she would have been upstairs in a flash. As it is, I self-administer first aid. It's easy to make a cold compress when the water comes out of the taps like ice. I think I've done a good job, so it's surprising to see how swollen my nose and left eye are in the morning. I look like I've been on the receiving end of a serious thumping.

While I'm doing some tough-guy gangster talk into the mirror—you ought to see the other guy, etc.—I notice that I really need a shave. Like really overdue need. Exactly how to go about that is the sort of thing I would have asked my dad if I'd had a clue he was going to leave us. Even though everything else on the bathroom shelf, from headache pills to tampons, has detailed instructions and warnings, razors don't. I don't want to risk slicing off my top lip, but there's no way I can ask my mother—that'd just be rubbing salt into the absent-father wound. Maybe there's a product along the lines of "my sucky little first razor" with step-by-step illustrations for klutzes. Or maybe not. I'll just add straggly, raised-by-wolves facial hair to my long list of charms.

Well used to my clumsiness, my mother gives an absent-minded "oh, darling" when she sees me. She guesses— "tripped over your pants," "fell out of bed," "opened the window in your face"—and nods when I tell her what happened. "Full marks for originality there," she says, ruffling my hair on her way out.

When I arrive at school, Mr. Pittney takes one look at me and asks me to follow him. After I finally convince him that I'm not being bullied, he assumes a more gentle expression and starts asking me how things are at home. I tell him the truth: as well as can be expected in the pretty dire circumstances, which include our sudden loss of fortune, my mother's growing Radiohead habit...But he cuts me short. Ushering me out, he assures me that listening to the radio is quite safe and that his door is always open. He closes it on me while I'm still wondering if I can ask such a mustached person about shaving without it seeming like I'm ridiculing him. "Do you know how to use a razor, Mr. Pittney?" "Got any tips on shaving, Mr. Pittney?"

Nah, it'd never work.

In the classroom corridor at the end of the day, there's a new mad energy zipping around like a snitch. People are yapping, whooping, laughing, yelling. Talking about limos and dresses and dates. A flyer about the year-nine social has just gone up. I search the crowd for another unexcited face: Lou. Thank you. She comes over.

"It's the first school dance in two years. Thus the hysteria level," she says. "The last one got busted when someone tipped off the police about drug use in the school."

"What did they find?"

"Not much, but we got a dodgy rep, anyway. And the local paper ran an 'underage drug-fueled orgy' sort of headline, so that was pretty funny."

"Will you go?" I ask.

"Not unless they make it compulsory," she says.

"Same," I say. But I'm thinking, not unless I can go with Estelle.

And tickets are twenty bucks—another reminder that I need a job, in case I do end up going.

My locker has been tagged again. That's another group I'm growing to know and love: the would-be homies who never have a fat Sharpie far from their grimy paws. But it's just about impossible to get mad with people dumb enough to leave their brand name at the crime scene. The

"FBK" crew guy gives me a reserved nod. I reserve-nod him back.

Reaching into my locker, I notice there's an alarming amount of wrist and forearm emerging from my gray shirtsleeves and sweater. I could do with a couple of sizes up, but when we bought this during the holidays it was a good fit, with room for growing. I look down. Pants much too short as well. This is good. Facial hair, swollen nose, black eye, clothes that don't fit—the whole cool thing is coming along nicely.

When I let myself in the front door, I can hear muffled shouting coming from the back of the house. I drop my bag and head for the kitchen. As I open the door, ready to spring into attack if necessary, my mother holds up her hand in a *wait there* sign. *Amnesiac* is playing in the background, and a young woman is pointing at an empty kitchen chair, sobbing, "And this wedding is *not* just about me, and my dress, and my cake, and my mother. Thank god I found out what a petty monster you are before it was too late." She glances up at my mother, who is nodding her calm approval. Then the woman stands up and kicks the chair over. "Bastard!" I gather the empty chair is her soon-to-be ex-fiancé. She bursts into tears and flings her arms around my mother.

Another one bites the dust.

>><<

Howard and I turn into the Edinburgh Gardens for a few laps of the big oval. He's dragging his paws a bit but managing to keep up.

We've been running for nearly an hour, and I still can't figure out how to persuade my mother to stop putting her clients off the idea of marriage. She's shooting herself in the foot, but who am I to lay down the law? Isn't it obvious that people have to go through with a wedding in order to need a wedding cake?

When I get home, my mother is happily singing along to "No Surprises," possibly her favorite Radiohead song.

"Did she change her mind? Is she ordering the cake?"

"Oh, no," she replies vaguely.

"Then how come you're singing? Haven't you just lost another customer?"

"Yes, but she was going to order the Rambling Rose."

The Rambling Rose is the most expensive cake in the range. Three tiers, covered in handmade pink chocolate roses and marzipan ribbons.

"But not anymore?"

"But only because she's not getting married anymore. She loved it!"

"That's . . . great."

I go upstairs for a shower. She's deluded, maybe in need of professional counseling. What should I do? My dad would know what to do. But if he were here, she wouldn't be having the meltdown. And he's not, so it's up to me. I don't want to go back down there and be the grown-up. I prefer being the kid, with parents doing the hard stuff.

>> <<

Stirring the stew, I try to channel my dad's tone: firm but humorous. I take a deep breath of the tomatoey, garlicky steam, and leap in.

"You can't keep talking people out of getting married."

"I just want them to consider the pros and cons."

"You're going overboard on the cons. It's not your job. Your job is the cake."

"I need to get to know them so I can plan the right cake. And then how can I give them an ethical cake if I think they're making a huge mistake?"

"You're dumping a whole antimarriage thing on them."

"No, I'm not."

"All you need from them is the date of the wedding and the number of guests, and then get them to choose the cake they like from the pictures."

I'm speaking to her back.

"And that chair business—give me a break—you're not some daytime TV shrink."

She serves the rice. Expression: neutral. She's thinking; it's sinking in. I hope.

13

When I get home from school the next day, she's had a stack of promotional flyers printed at the Officeworks around the corner. I breathe a sigh of relief. Something I said last night must have penetrated. She's back on board the sane train.

But only for a minute. She wants me to take a bunch of flyers to the staff room at school. Is she kidding? No. And it's hard to argue with her logic. Teachers are always getting married. It's like their number one hobby or something.

I'm pretty sure being the PR boy for a wedding-cake business is another rung on the social-suicide ladder, so I make sure I'm in early the next morning to jam some flyers under the staff room door. And that's it. I'll try to get rid of some more at the shops after school. Relief at getting the job done without being spotted is short-lived when Jayzo grabs a handful of flyers from my bag at the lockers.

"Are you having a party, jerk-off?" he asks. But then, proof that he can actually read, he says, "What's this lame-arsed cake business got to do with you?"

I try ignoring him. Great tactic in theory. Practical success rate? For me, about one in twenty. He uses a flyer on me like a face-washer. It really hurts my bruised and battered face. "I asked you a question."

"It's my mother's business," I say through gritted teeth.

"Is that right?"

He folds the flyer carefully and puts it in his pocket, sneering.

As he walks off, Lou says, "I think he likes you."

I have to introduce Lou to Fred.

On the way home, I stop at all the likely shops and drop off flyers. When I get to Phrenology, the bald guy, Ali, is sitting on a bar stool in the window talking to an old guy. So I go in and wait.

It's a comfortable, homey café. Red concrete floor, long marble counter, cookies in huge laboratory jars, wooden chair all-sorts, cakes on tiered stands, mismatched flower-patterned cups and saucers in a pigeonhole grid mounted on the wall, yellow tulips in a blue enamel coffeepot, blackboard menu, lightbulbs hanging from long looped cords, a deep wooden crate painted lettuce green and half full of baguettes. I want to work here.

Two cool mothers sit deep in conversation while their little kids turn cake into a spitty mess—wearing some, eating some, and smearing some around.

Ali notices me and throws an impatient look at the girl behind the counter washing glasses. "How can we help you?" he asks, catching her attention. I recognize the dark red hair before she turns to me with a glare of recognition. It's Estelle's friend Janie. She wipes her hands on the black wrap apron.

"What can I get you?" she asks with a smile that's polite on the surface but flipping me off underneath.

I fake concentration on the cakes and pastries piled in a glass display cabinet on the counter. "They look good."

Janie rolls her fierce black-rimmed eyes. "Would you like to choose one?" then dropping her voice, "Or would you prefer me to read your mind?"

"I've come about work," I say. If I'd had any money on me, I would have chickened out, bought a cake, and run.

"He's here about a job," she calls in Ali's direction, turning back to the sink.

Ali is about thirty-five. Black jeans, black sweater, black stubble. Tall, tough-looking. He'd be a perfectly believable bouncer. He looks at me with such focus as I head over, I feel as though I have a large sign hanging around my neck that says:

"Hi, I'm Dan," I say, as a dad-imprint reminder floats to the surface: make eye contact, shake hands. His grip is like a tourniquet.

"How old are you?"

"Nearly fifteen."

"Come back after your birthday."

I'm expecting this one. "I'm prepared to be trained free of charge until I turn fifteen. I really need a job."

"Have you got any experience?"

"Not in the area."

My only job has been an abortive paperboy stint when I was twelve, where Dad ended up driving me half the time.

"What makes you think you're suited to working in a café?"

"I love food, and I'm interested in the service industry."

I've rehearsed all this, but it comes off sounding like something out of *Job Interviews for Dummies*. Is he buying it?

"Can you handle a boss who shouts occasionally?"

It's more like all the time, according to Mrs. Da Silva, so I'm prepared for this, too.

"I'm used to it. My dad used to yell quite a bit."

"But he's stopped?"

"Kind of. He doesn't live with us anymore."

His considering look makes me babble on. I hope he doesn't think my dad's "inside" or something. "So it's just me and Mum now. Mum and I. She has a food business, too. Wedding cakes." I pull a flyer from my backpack. "Maybe...would it be okay if I put this up in your window?"

He looks it over. "Sure. Okay, I'll give you a paid trial. If you handle it well, we can talk about part-time work when you turn fifteen. Breakages get taken out of your pay."

I'm coming in for the morning shift on Saturday, seven until twelve thirty. Fantastic. When I tell him I can help out by taking home any leftover food, he just smiles and heads out the back.

As soon as he's out of range, Janie comes over. Foolishly, I smile, imagining she's going to congratulate me on getting a job. But she says, "Stop staring at my friend all the time in class. She thinks you're a creep."

>> «

The winter days are still so short. It's nearly five o'clock, and the wind is scribbling the trees' bare branches against a darkening sky. Following my dragon-breath home along the puddled sidewalk, I worry about the frequency of my Estelle glances in class. I honestly thought I had a lid on that. Does she really think I'm a creep, or is that just Janie's helpful take on the situation? Has Estelle actually called me a "creep"? Or has she said something like, "It's

89

a bit 'creepy' when people look at you in class"? There's quite a difference.

When I get home, the phone is ringing and my mother's not home. Despite my jostling worries, I remember to answer the right way. "*I Do* Wedding Cakes, how may I help you?" The voice at the other end sounds like someone my own age: "How may I help you, dickbrain?" There's the sound of two people snorting with laughter. And they hang up. Thank you, Jayzo.

My heart is racing, my face burning. The phone rings again. "Yes?" I bark down the line. It's my mother.

"Dan, how many times are we going to go over this? Please answer with the business name. You're so keen on telling me how to run the show, but you have to do your bit, too."

She's calling to let me know she's at a small-business seminar at the library and there's some food in the fridge for dinner.

When the phone rings again ten minutes later, I figure it's her checking up on me. But no, it's another prank call. "You may help me by walking under a truck," a girl sputters. More laughing and another hang up. A few minutes later another call—gee, the gang's all there. "You 'do' wedding cakes? That's disgusting." The high-end wit keeps on coming. Four more calls in the next hour and that's it. I put on the answering machine. Surprise, surprise, my amusing classmates' calls peter out. I'm fuming. I'm embarrassed. I need to talk to Fred, but when I call, the Gazelle tells me he's at debate club.

Before I get ready for bed, I work out some anger with a good weights session. Why am I persisting despite my aching arms and aching face? Getting stronger and looking better is now imperative. I want to be able to stand up to Jayzo—and his prank-calling band of hyenas—including thumping him, if it comes to that. Also against all odds and any likelihood, I keep imagining the unimaginable that I will somehow go to the dance with Estelle. Despite knowing it is utterly stupid and I am utterly stupid, given the latest "creep" update, images of us together keep invading my thoughts.

I hear her moving in the attic, push on through the pain barrier, and reenter the shame zone as I remember my second visit to the attic.

14

The last weekend of the holidays we moved in, Estelle and her parents were going away. She and her mother were fighting, as usual—Estelle didn't want to go. I waited until they'd left, and then another hour, in case of an essential-item-forgotten return trip, before I decided the coast was clear.

She hadn't replaced the box of books over the hatch cover, so I knew my first visit was undiscovered. I pushed the packing boxes away from the hole between my side and Estelle's side of the attic, putting the cord in my pocket to reposition them on my way out. I was being sneaky and deliberate. It gets worse.

A figure stepped toward me as I entered the space. As quickly as I gasped in terror and surprise, I recognized the looming shape as my own reflection. Estelle had moved one of the big mirrors. Calming down, I scoped the space and headed for the desk. I'd seen something during that first visit that my feet were making a beeline for. I still hadn't consciously decided to go to the dark side. But it sure looked like I was heading that way. It was a stack of notebooks I'd remembered seeing, and they were still there.

Carefully checking exactly how they were positioned on the desk, and keeping them in order, my black heart gave the green light to my reading Estelle's diaries.

She'd started writing them in grade six, and was still going. She was bigger on highs and lows than day-to-day detail, although, like me, she is a chronic list-maker. I can't offer any excuse for doing what I did, but I can say I read so fast it was as though someone had plugged a cord into my forehead and clicked an icon to download data. My eyes scanned those pages at the most feverish rate imaginable. I'd race back to the top of each page, unable to believe I'd read everything in the first rush of blood. But I always had. I was as thirsty for those words as it is possible to be. I needed to know her, and here was a foul means dangled before me. I failed the test completely. I hardly struggled. I knew what I was doing was morally reprehensible. And still I did it. All's fair in love and war, right?

Right?

I felt empathy for eleven-year-old Estelle's feelings on her parents' imminent overseas trip—I remember thinking exactly the same sort of stuff:

*It's official. I HATE my mum and dad. They're
probably not even my real parents. Let them see how
much they miss me when I'm DEAD. See if I care if
they go to Paris for work. AS IF it would matter for
me to miss two weeks of CRAP school. I'll probably
catch meningococcal virus and then they'll be sorry,
but it will be WAY TOO LATE.*

Since the "creep" episode, I take pathetic vengeful pleasure remembering Estelle's falling-out with Janie in year
seven. I try not to dwell on the fact that I've earned the
epithet a thousand times over:

*Janie Bacon better get her friends SORTED OUT. She
likes me or not, and I couldn't care less either way. She'll
soon find out she can't play her petty little HOT and
COLD guessing games with me. She needs a wake-up
call BIG TIME. And I'm just the one to do it before she
turns into a giant, friend-slaying bitch for good.*

An involuntary goofy smile hits me when I think about
her cloud sandwiches:

*I'll scoop off a sweet piece of that cloud and put it on
some bread. I'll float another slice on top, so gently
the cloud won't fly away, and when I bite down and
stray wisps whoosh out the sides, I'll lick them up.
They'll taste like atomized Turkish delight. I'll call*

it a floating sandwich. First it will make me dream
of flying, then it will make me fly.

I take a break between sets with the weights and visit the inventory for the millionth time:

Our bands in common are Hot Chip, TV on the Radio, and Kings of Leon.

We both hate humid weather and long-haul flights and most fantasy writing.

We're both list- and chart-makers. She catalogs all her "likes" and "dislikes"—bands, books, films, food: In year six her favorite sweets were musk sticks and savory junk was Twisties. In year nine it's sour worms and salt and vinegar potato chips. In the hot drinks zone it was hot chocolate with pink marshmallows, and now it's mochaccino. Film was *10 Things I Hate About You*, and now it's *Donnie Darko* and Baz Luhrmann's *Romeo + Juliet*.

At the time of the snooping, before we'd even met, I realized that just as my regard for her grew with every word I read, hers for me would surely diminish in far greater proportion if she ever found out what I had done.

Knowing her now, even so slightly, only makes what I did seem more horrible.

I've paid a high price for knowledge that should have been earned, not stolen. It's a bad bargain, and one from which I can't see an escape. Like all good traps, climbing in was easy, getting out might prove to be impossible.

15

"You know who *is* a good guy?" my mother asks me over oatmeal, in a tone suggesting we've just been talking about who's *not* a good guy, which we haven't.

"No."

"Thom Yorke. He is a truly good guy." Radiohead's singer, songwriter. The unnatural interest isn't going away.

"What makes you think that?"

"Because he's passionate, Dan; he cares passionately about things. You just have to watch him performing to see it. He looks like he's going to burst every blood vessel in his head..."

"What's so good about that?"

"He's also an environmental activist." She stirs sugar

into her tea, a dreamy expression on her face. "He cares about climate change. He went to the Copenhagen Summit, for god's sake! He's helping the planet."

"Okay." I'm putting my lunch together. I've got to get out of here.

"And he's around my age, did you know that?"

"No."

"Yep. So, why didn't I end up with him, instead of your father?"

Who knows the right answer to that one? Er—you live on different continents...? You don't know him...? He's short and you're tall...?

I don't point out that I'm the result of her breeding with her reject husband. I don't feel like much of a consolation.

$$\gg \ll$$

It's clear I have to protect my mother from the prank phone calls in her current fragile state, so I do something I've never done before in my school history. When Mr. Pittney finishes morning homeroom with a rhetorical, "That's it, then?" I stand up and speak in front of the whole class. Voluntarily. Not for assessment purposes. It's weird—I don't consciously decide to do it; it's as though I'm watching myself do something I have no power to stop, even though I know it's going to hurt.

I walk to the front of the class and hold up a flyer, my face growing red in a rush of embarrassed second thoughts. Too late now.

"This is my mother's business. She makes wedding cakes. She's having a hard time. My father walked out on us eight weeks ago. And he lost all our money. Or we didn't have any, or something. And so my mother has to make this business work, or we can't afford to...live. I'm not talking holidays or luxury vehicles, I'm talking food. So please do not ring this number unless you want a cake."

Pittney has obviously only been half listening, as usual.

"Thank you. Righto, so, I think if we, if anyone, that is, wants a wedding cake, we all know where to take our business. But no more advertisements in homeroom, thanks, Cereal."

"Cereill."

"Of course, Cereill."

Estelle is looking at me curiously. Add inappropriate blurting of private family matters to the list. Jayzo is sneering and aggressive, but I hold eye contact with him in as threatening a manner as I can manage. He'd better get the message or I'm going to have to do something more drastic. What that might be, I have no idea. Until the muscles develop, sharp words are the only other thing in the arsenal.

Jayzo yells out, "Who's up for some pus and raw brains?" Nice. Now he's trying to make me faint, hitting me where it hurts. Lou shoots me a sympathetic look. "What about some raw liver and snot?" Jayzo asks.

I make it back to my seat just in time, through sniggering and Mr. Pittney's confused "settle downs."

>> <<

That night there are five more prank calls. Speaking up seems only to have inspired the few people who hadn't already called. I answer the phone and tell my mother they're wrong numbers.

Maybe it shouldn't be such a big deal, but it is. I hate using the polite business voice and saying the stupid business name, only to cop inane abuse, knowing it's someone I'm going to see at school in the morning but not knowing quite who. The anonymity turns the whole class into enemies. If someone smiles, it feels like mockery. The calls go on for a couple of more nights.

At school I get called "cake boy," arguably no better or worse than "dickhead," or "cereal," but I feel more exposed than before. I've appealed to people's better nature. I've made myself conspicuous by telling them about my life, and now they're clubbing me over the head with it.

I'm full of pointless anger toward my mother for her stupid business intruding on my stupid life. I know it's really my father who started the ball rolling down this bad hill, but he's not around to blame, and besides, I can't be any more pissed off with him than I already am. Bashing away at the back of my skull is the obvious: It's not about my parents, it's me, and how I'm—not—handling things.

Life in our cold house grows colder. I barely speak to my mother. And she hardly notices. I guess she's silently

99

communing with Thom Yorke. She and Oliver share an occasional bottle of wine, but as far as I know she doesn't see any of her old friends.

I've decided my mother's probably right about Oliver. He seems like a pretty average guy who's unlikely to be up for random killings. He's got good taste in music, people who visit him leave unharmed, and there are no suspicious, freshly dug areas in the garden.

That's where he and I have our occasional talks. He tells me that the hedge running along the back of the house with the lemon-smelling flowers is daphne, and my window tree is a *Magnolia grandiflora*.

He doesn't mind when I ask him stuff, for example:

1. "Were you always cool?"
   He just laughed about that. For quite a while.

2. "What makes someone cool?"
   "Not what you'd think. Not the outward stuff. The coolest thing is just to be authentically yourself."

3. "What if you're a psychopath?"
   "If you're a psychopath, sure, try to be someone else."

4. "What do you think about someone deciding they're gay when they're thirty-nine?"
   "It's one year better than doing it at forty. And he's being authentically himself."

5. "How do you think my mum's coping?"
   "Not fantastic, but not terrible."

6. "What about the Thom Yorke thing?"
   "It's transitional. She's not crazy. It's like eating choc-olate when you feel sad. But heaps healthier. And she's got good taste."

He gets along well with Howard and offers to walk him when I've got café shifts after school, which I do now on Wednesdays and Fridays, up for review in a week, when I turn fifteen.

He greets me by saying, "Hey, man," but it doesn't sound stupid when he says it. When he suggests I could do with a shave, I find myself saying, "I don't know how." So that's how I first come to visit the stables, because he says I can watch him shave. It seems a bit personal, I know, but I think, *what the hell*, there's no one else around offering.

He has converted the stables into one huge space. It's lined with tall bookshelves filled with books, CDs, and DVDs. In one corner there's a kitchen, in another, a bath-room. Up one set of stairs is a big sleeping platform, up another, an office area. There's a long table with twelve chairs around it, a giant square *U* of sofas, and a massive wall-mounted screen. His bike hangs on the wall like a piece of art, and there's a lot of actual art as well. One look around and I know this is exactly the sort of place I want to have when I'm older.

"You like it?" Oliver asks.

I nod. "How come you're here?"

"You know Adelaide and my gran were friends, and I used to do the gardening here, as a student job? One day I asked her if I could rent the stables."

"Were they like this?"

"No, they were a mess. Broken roof. Lots of birds. We worked out a deal where I'd fix them up instead of paying rent. And she liked the security of having someone else around."

"Did you know she was leaving them to you?"

"No idea."

Shaving doesn't look that hard. Lather up. Stretch tight the piece of your face being shaved using appropriate contortions. Move the razor up, down, or sideways, always moving it in the direction of the handle, not in the direction of the blades. Oliver hands me a new razor, wishes me luck, and sends me on my way. Maybe he'll break up with his girlfriend, fall for my mother, and move inside—then I can live in the stables. Brilliant. I imagine cool, casual gatherings with Estelle and friends. I only have Fred and Lou in the friends department, of course, but small details don't need to spoil a perfectly good fantasy.

Work at Phrenology is harder than it looks from the outside. In the first couple of shifts I break a few things, but not too many. I get to know Ali's temper firsthand. He's an impatient perfectionist, and insults fly around the place like pepper, but he's just as quick to cool down.

I'm learning how to use the bench-top dishwasher, and to wash by hand when that's full—squeaking clean glasses, no trace of lipstick. I get the hang of sweeping methodically, every chair up on a table, starting around all the skirting boards and counter edges and working my way into the middle of the floor. Ali goes ballistic when he sees my first attempt at wiping a table.

"What's this?" he growls, running a finger through the beaded smear I've left on the surface.

"I don't know…" I haven't got a clue what I've done wrong.

"It's laziness. It's blindness. It's sloppy. It's out the door if you ever do it again."

He shows me how to do it properly. Scalding hot cloth, wrung out till it's nearly dry. Catch all the crumbs and goop in your hand; don't sweep them off the table onto the floor.

"And the essential ingredient?" he asks with a look of dire threat.

I'm mute.

"Elbow grease. Work it! Put some muscle into it."

I practice that first week until my back is ready to break. Then I've got it. Never need reminding again. So just when I'm used to Ali's barking, it stops. We spray and wipe all the tables at the end of the day with a eucalyptus oil and water mixture. That freshness blends with the morning smells. My first Saturday morning shift, I meet Ali's mother, Anne. She starts cooking at six. I walk into the warm baking smells of lemon peel, pistachios, walnuts, honey, and rosewater. Mingling with the smell of cakes is the first coffee of the morning. Ali is the only one allowed near the coffee machine.

I clear glasses and crockery, learning how to move around the tables and chairs and people and not trip over myself. It's like working out dance steps. You're moving quickly all the time, but always hesitating for a fraction of a beat to check the way is clear. "Behind you," we say over and over again, avoiding collisions with other people weaving through the same space.

Anne cooks with ease and grace, usually working with her friend Irena. They chat and laugh as they roll, peel, pound, and stir. It looks as though they've been doing what they do every day forever—so different from my mother's focused, frowning, scientific approach.

Phrenology is thriving, but *I Do* Wedding Cakes is not managing to get off the ground. Despite our recent rational discussion, my mother has counseled two more would-be customers out of getting married. And they're just the ones I know about. Who knows how many others she's put off.

Mrs. Da Silva is not surprised when I tell her about my mother's latest losses.

"Marriage is the problem, Dan. And there's no getting

around it if your business is wedding cakes. Perhaps we can move her gently into some other special occasion cakes."

"Do you think you could mention it? She's a bit sick of me trying to tell her stuff like that."

"Certainly," she nods. "Look after the shop while I get Howard some bones?"

I stand behind the counter, staring into space. If my mother can't make a go of the business, what does that mean for us? My job at Phrenology isn't a sure thing yet. But even if it happens, it's not going to be enough to kick a hole in things like utility bills, which now come twice, the second time on red stationery.

Mrs. Da Silva comes out with the bones and gives me a bag of mixed sweets—she makes them up herself and sells them for fifty cents—for minding the shop. I protest, but she's a determined woman.

When I get home, finishing the last musk stick, my mother is sitting at the kitchen table crying. Big, snotty, gasping crying. She's been at it for a while, judging by her blotchy, swollen face.

"I thought you were working," she says.

"I've finished. It's dinnertime."

"I haven't made anything."

I'm starving. I know I should be offering sympathy and comfort. I know she's going through a hard time. I feel sorry, but not for her. For myself. I'm working hard. I'm copping it about her business at school, while all she does is send customers away. I understand about posttraumatic stress disorder in theory, but all I can think is that I want my easy life and my happy mother back. And dinner.

So like a prize brat I say, "That'd be right."

It's like I've slapped her.

"What did you say? *What* did you just say?"

At least I recognize that it's time to shut up. A sudden, white-hot fury replaces her tears. She is shouting through the sobs and hiccups.

"Do you realize what utter complete *shit* my life is at the moment? Do you know we could be living on the *streets* if we didn't have the use of this house? Because we have no *savings*, if I get sick we're . . . and this place is a *pigsty*. I keep the kitchen clean, but you haven't lifted a *finger* to help."

"You haven't asked."

"Because I expect someone who is *nearly fifteen* to have half a clue about things and to be able to put dirty clothes in the laundry and not leave a trail of his belongings around the house, and just *be here* occasionally to help out."

"I'm only out because I'm trying to make some *money*. Because I have to save up to go to my own social and even buy some clothes that actually *fit* me."

Crap. Why did I mention the social? I'm not even going to the stupid thing. But she's in a frenzy, and nothing I'm saying is sinking in anyway.

"Don't you dare shout at me. I'm trying to make some money, too. And it's bloody hard."

"It wouldn't be so 'bloody hard' if you stopped sending customers away."

"I don't! They just change their mind about getting married."

"Or maybe they recognize a crazy psycho when they meet one, and go somewhere else for their stupid cake!"

I walk out. I can't handle it. I stamp through the house, longing to smash something, but restrict myself to slamming my door, opening it again, and slamming it again. A patch of plaster from above the door falls, settling on the large pile of recycled socks and boxers I've been dressing from lately. I lie down and pick up the weights. I'm doing them twice a day and can lift them easily now. Adrenaline pumps through my system; I've never managed so many repetitions before.

><·><

My mother knocks on my door.

"Dan?" She tries the handle. It's locked.

"Go away."

"I've made you a sandwich."

"I don't want it." What am I, five? She must know it's a lie, anyway.

I hear her putting a plate down outside the door, with a huge sigh. I'm still burning with self-righteous rage and a petty impulse tells me not to eat it. My mother doesn't seem to realize that things are every bit as bad for me as they are for her. Does she even know or ask how I'm doing? Is it fun for me being pulled out of my life and dumped in this cold, dreary museum?

I've always assumed that me being around means my mother has to cope, and she has to think her life's okay. That is clearly not the case. It makes me feel hollow and hopeless.

"Thom Yorke and I obviously aren't enough, Howard."

He gives me the inscrutable psychotherapist look: You figure it out.

"Well, I can't. That's why I'm talking to a dog. And imagining a dog is talking to me."

He turns away, huffy. Now the whole world is against me.

"I'm sorry. I didn't mean to disparage your species."

He comes back over and settles himself next to me. You could interpret that as him wanting some physical warmth, but it feels more like being forgiven. I don't know exactly when it happened, but he's my dog and I'm his human.

There's a bump from above. The unattainable one. So close, but never farther away...

16

Revisiting the list:

1. Kiss Estelle.

   Okay, at least I've met her. She thinks I'm a creep. And that's without her knowing I've read her diaries. Unless we somehow fall over, exactly aligned, lips to lips, and gravity causes the pressure, or we find ourselves in a darkened room and through a series of Shakespearean ID muddles she thinks she's kissing someone else, I can't see how this is ever going to happen.

2. Get a job.

   Got a job, probably.
   Still in financial crisis mode.

3. Cheer my mother up.
   Failing. She's a nutcase.

4. Try not to be a complete loser.
   Failing completely. Am a complete loser.

5. Should talk to my father when he calls.
   Still can't face asking him, how could you leave us like this? The other thing that I wake up thinking is, you're not who I thought you were. Did you even love us in the first place?

6. Figure out how to be good.
   Failing utterly.

17

My mother and I are mostly skirting around each other. Anytime we go beyond talking about food, or what time I'm going to be home, we end up fighting and neither of us wants that. She needs some "happy family" illusion, and I just can't be bothered fighting.

And I'd like to ask her more about my father, but I can't. I wish I could talk to her about how I don't want to see him, and yet equally, I miss him. How I wonder a lot about him being gay. Did he always know it? Or was it unexpected, like a fit of sneezing? Or is there such a thing as sexuality amnesia? It's so confusing.

Under the weight of everything that remains unspoken,

the niggling *your father called* message surfaces every few days.

"Tell him to stop calling."

"Tell him yourself."

"I don't want to speak to him."

"Neither do I, particularly. And I don't want him to think I'm not passing along his messages, so please just call him."

I'm not budging on this one.

"He'll give up eventually."

"Don't forget he's left that present for your birthday."

"I don't even know where it is."

Howard looks up from his bed of cardigans, head tilted skeptically to one side.

I scratch Howard's ears, trying to figure out how the hell he knows I'm lying, as I half listen to my mother.

"It's just... there's no cash flow at the moment. I've got you something little, but it's not going to be like other birthdays."

"No kidding."

A disappointed look from Howard.

I know I'm being mean, but I can't seem to stop it. It's like the editing equipment on my bile has packed up. It's better not to talk.

It's mostly because I'm avoiding my mother that I go to the after-school reading group. That, and I know Estelle goes.

And Lou says, "You'll love it—it's like English class minus the morons."

The youngest English teacher, Ms. Griffin, runs it. She has red hair, and her ears and cheeks and chin turn pink with enthusiasm.

I glance over at Estelle a few times, and, unnervingly, she looks up each time and sees me looking at her, so I immediately look away. Now I'm vying with Ms. Griffin for the pink face prize. But it's like Estelle's a magnet and I'm metal, and the second I stop concentrating on *not* looking, I'm looking at her again. Now Janie and Estelle are both looking at me and I can read Janie's thought bubble: "Stop staring at my friend, you creep."

Ms. Griffin reads aloud from a Raymond Carver short story. It's clean writing that I like straightaway. The story's called "Nobody Said Anything"; it's about a kid who lies to his mother, skips school, jerks off, and then what happens when he goes fishing. The discussion is about how some compromises are a mess, and how everyone has to go through problems their own way, and on their own. I don't say anything, but boy, can I relate.

At the end I say good-bye to Lou and walk off in the same direction as Estelle and Janie. It's the perfect opportunity to walk along with them—just be myself, join in, etc., but of course I don't. They talk quietly as they walk. I feel obliged to clear my throat loudly in case they don't realize I'm right behind them. When they see I'm there, they stop talking, so I cross the road and walk on the opposite sidewalk. I feel acutely conspicuous, because we're taking exactly the same route home, and when we get there I have to cross back over the road.

"We don't bite, you know," Janie snarls, as they disappear through Estelle's shiny crimson front door.

In the kitchen Mrs. Da Silva and my mother are drinking peppermint tea, and my mother looks a fraction less frazzled than she has been lately. I start getting some food.

"I'm sorry about the late notice, but the daughter who promised is snowed under..." says Mrs. Da Silva.

"Tomorrow's fine," my mother says. "I'll bake it tonight and frost it first thing in the morning. It'll be ready to pick up anytime from noon."

Looking at me, she explains, "Mary's asked me to cook a wake cake."

Mrs. Da Silva gives me a little wink. I nearly choke on my banana and peanut butter sandwich. It's genius—my mother can't talk a dead person out of dying.

"The second cousin I told you about," Mrs. Da Silva says, with a philosophical grimace.

"Cancer of the liver," I remember.

"Swift. And she was eighty-eight. So..." Mrs. Da Silva folds her arms across her chest, satisfied there are worse ways to go. She's wearing an orange sari today, with a purple polar fleece vest. She's mad for the polar fleece.

"Dan, could you please pick some violets?" my mother asks.

"Your mother is making a rich chocolate cake with rum-soaked raisins, frosted with a chocolate ganache, and sprinkled with frosted violets and slivers of gold leaf."

"And you're thinking sixty servings?" my mother checks.

"Perhaps we'd better make it eighty," says Mrs. Da Silva. "It's Russell's family—they're a greedy lot."

My mother starts getting some cake tins down to show Mrs. Da Silva the exact size the cake will be, and I go out with a bowl to pick the violets.

They're growing all along the base of the daphne hedge, and there are heaps of flowers out.

I start at the end where our garden borders Estelle's. When I hear voices, I step in closer, jamming myself between two big shrubs right next to the fence. Eavesdropping is nothing to someone who's low enough to read a diary. It's Estelle and Janie. Janie's having a cigarette; that must be why they're hiding out next to the fence. (Smoking is on Estelle's "Things that disgust me" list.) I just hope Mrs. Da Silva stays in the kitchen for a bit longer.

When I hear my name—well, "cake boy"—my ears strain so hard I forget to breathe.

It's Janie who says, "What about cake boy?"

Estelle laughs. "Are you kidding?"

"Why? Why not?" says Janie.

"He's just not right," says Estelle.

Right for what?

"We'd have to swear him to secrecy," says Janie.

"I suppose he could be okay..." Estelle thinks I could be okay. Yes! But what for?

"He's not the sort you'd suspect."

"The element of surprise." Estelle's trying it on for size, I can tell she's just about convinced.

"Do you think we could persuade him?"

"Maybe."

Maybe nothing. Estelle could persuade me to do anything.

"Definitely," says Janie. "He's hot for you in a big way."

"Shut up."

No, she's right.

"Well, he never stops staring at you. I told him you think he's a creep."

"I never said that."

Aha!

"Sure you did."

"Janie, I did not."

Oh, joy.

"Well, he is."

"Anyway, why don't you ask him? You work with the guy."

Hmm. She could have fought back a bit, surely?

"Does he have it in him to kill someone, though? That's what we need to decide."

Kill someone? I nearly fall over. In the shocked instant I take this at face value, a range of enticing images floods through me—the thrilling possibility of Estelle using her persuasive powers to lure me, one chilling yet seductive step at a time, to life on the wrong side of the law. Could I resist, or would I turn into a compliant puppet in her supple hands? The latter for sure.

Howard comes barking his head off out the back door, heading straight for me, followed by Mrs. Da Silva. I emerge from my hiding place with as casual an air as I can muster.

"There are plenty, Dan, over here," she says, pointing to the violets.

To her complete puzzlement I silently sprint as far away as I can from the fence before answering, "Thanks." With any luck they won't guess they've been overheard.

I'm wondering what the hell they were talking about as I bring the violets inside, and register my mother has just said we are invited in next door for a drink tonight.

"Don't you have to cook the wake cake?"

"Yes, but these have to soak before I can do much." She points at the raisins. "And the violets have to be washed and dried before I can start on them."

"Do I have to come?"

"Unless you've got a compelling reason not to, yes, you do."

"Why?"

"Because it's a polite, neighborly response to a polite, neighborly invitation."

Seeing my glum face, she continues. "The girl is in your class, isn't she? Or your year level, at least?"

"Yeah."

"When we get there, stand up straight and try not to be so morose, if you can manage it."

We're on their doorstep fifteen minutes later. My mother has put on lipstick. I'm trying to boost my confidence by talking to myself: "She doesn't think I'm a creep, she doesn't think I'm a creep," but a parenthesis keeps sneaking in (but she would if she found out what I've done...), followed by another one (but she never needs to find out...).

Estelle's mother lets us in, and under the introductions and greetings, I check out their house. A breathtaking contrast to Adelaide's, it's had the guts stripped out of it. Most of the walls are gone and everything is painted white. Just as Adelaide's house is choking with more junk than you can imagine, this house is almost empty, except for not very many pieces of modern furniture and art. It's warm and smells beautiful. Estelle's mother, Vivien, is thin with very white skin and very red lips, wearing a complicated black dress that looks as though it is trying to disguise the fact that it's made for humans. Her hair is cut into weird asymmetry. She's a curator. In the middle of a show. Frantic! So sorry not to have been in touch earlier! The father is called Peter. I've never seen or heard him. He disappears soon after introducing himself, talking into his cell and throwing a phony apologetic look in our direction.

Estelle troops in wearing her school uniform and a resigned expression, carrying a large, shallow bowl of potato chips.

There's another plate of food the mothers are nibbling from, and soon they are happily nattering away about white anchovies and an obscure restaurant they've both been to in Rome.

Estelle is looking at me with some concentration— perhaps wondering, is he our killer? And I'm hoping for enlightenment about that conversation. Is it a metaphor? Code language? Are they putting on a play? Do they want me to eradicate some pests?

As usual around the unattainable one, I'm confused and tongue-tied. But for a change, Estelle is interested in talking to me.

She asks me about work, and about how I like school. I manage to stumble and mumble my way through answering some questions, and then remember my dad dissing someone they know who never speaks, except in response to direct questions. He's one of my father's top five bores. I do not want to be like that guy, so I snap out of it.

I tell her about the thrift store, and Howard, and with a wobble of conscience, ask her about music, knowing we'll connect over TV on the Radio and Hot Chip, and we do. So after only a little bit of plonking through wet cement in clown shoes, I'm actually enjoying myself. In fact, I feel as though I could look into those eyes—dark, stormy blue— and talk about anything forever.

The social comfort is short-lived. My mother starts making moves to go, then says, with absolutely no warning, "Oh, you two can go to the year-nine dance together. That's handy."

My deepest wish sits there on the floor, as unprotected and squirmy as a little turtle out of its shell. A rush of heat to my face feeds on itself and spreads. What is she thinking? Where did that come from?

Estelle says, very pointedly, "I'm probably already going with someone."

Estelle's father comes in just then, and they're all looking at my face as it burns on. He walks over and picks up a thermostat remote control. "Bit warm in here, is it?" he asks, pointing the thing nowhere in particular and clicking away.

My mother says, "I'm just talking about sharing a ride."

Vivien says, "Sounds like a good idea."

I say, "I might be going with someone, too."

Good strategy: When you're in a tight spot, dig yourself deeper.

My mother asks, "Who?"

"No one you know."

"Well, perhaps you can all share a ride together," she says with patronizing, exaggerated patience.

She and Vivien exchange a *teenagers, you can't say a thing right* smile, and we leave.

"Sorry if I embarrassed you back there," she says when we get home.

"I'd really appreciate it if you'd just stay the hell out of my business."

Oh, yes, because I'm handling it all so well. Or maybe not, in light of the current crises.

1. Attic temptation.

   Much as I am intrigued by the idea of Estelle as a heinous conspirator to murder, prepared to use me callously to achieve her evil goal, I am dying to know what Estelle and Janie were actually talking about. I begin to think about a third attic visit. Why not? I've already gone all the way in the bad stakes. What's one more tiny little peek going to matter? The moral slippery slope—wheeee.

2. Money worries.

   The nest-egg thing is eating me up. How can I provide any cushioning when I earn so little? Three shifts at Phrenology, crummy fifteen-year-old hourly rate as of my birthday next week, plus two shifts at the thrift store, zero hourly rate. But I can't just dump that, at least not until a respectable interval has passed. (Three months? Six months? And how am I going to work that one out?) Not enough time; not nearly enough

money. I've told Fred we can see a movie this weekend,
but that just seems like a money-wasting activity. And
I can't keep scabbing off my best friend.

3. Mother meanness—mine to her, not hers to me.
   I have to start being nicer to my mother, somehow
   find my sympathy for her again; I have it in theory. If
   someone were to tell me her story I'd feel sorry for her,
   no question. I just can't find it in practice. Why is it so
   impossible just to be pleasant?

4. Father call.
   I told my mother he'd give up calling eventually, but
   the idea terrifies me. The calls are a lifeline. I'm hang-
   ing on, just not ready to pull myself in yet. If he gives
   up, I drown. Down, down, down into the black water
   between our icebergs.

5. Howard limping.
   Sort of a subset of the money worries category. It means
   a vet visit. No idea how much that costs, but I bet it's
   heaps.

6. Need new clothes.
   Could also be considered a subset of money worries.
   Arms and legs sticking out of clothes, toes jammed in
   shoes. Replacing them is up to me. No more visits to
   the uniform shop asking them to put whatever on the

parents' account. I can probably get some casuals from the thrift store, but not sure on etiquette of buying from where you work.

Problems, responsibilities, frowns. It feels like a million years ago that all I had to worry about was beating ancient games on Nintendo, or getting homework done on time.

I decide I could do worse than speak to Oliver about some of this stuff.

18

When you watch someone shave, a barrier is broken down. It feels easy to talk to Oliver now.

I mostly need to ask him about clothes and money, so I'm as surprised as anyone to hear myself lead with, "What do you think about Estelle from next door?"

He gives me an assessing once-over.

"Out of your league, man, unless you do something about the look," he says.

"You said outward stuff doesn't make you cool."

"It's definitely not *the* thing, but it is *a* thing. It's one of those weird paradoxes life throws up—it can't make you cool, but it can make you uncool."

Now he tells me.

"What should I do?"

"Getting rid of the bum fluff was an excellent move. Now you need clothes that do you some favors, give you some edge. And the hair"—he shakes his own svelte locks—"I'm gonna be brutal, it needs a total rethink."

My hair? I haven't even given it a think, let alone a rethink. And that, possibly, is the nub of the problem. It's been months since the last haircut, and it's just hanging there. I do keep it clean. More or less. When I remember.

"We need Em."

"Hairdresser?"

"Girlfriend. She's a DJ, but she's pretty good at chopping into hair."

"When's she coming back?"

"Soon, I hope. You still working at the thrift store?"

"Yep."

"Those bags over there—it's stuff I don't wear anymore, right. How about you go through it, take what you want, and drop the rest off for me?"

"Thanks."

"Forget it. You're doing me a favor."

Oliver thinks a new school uniform can be acquired from lost property. I dump the old stuff there and pick up whatever someone else has been careless enough to lose. Swings and roundabouts, etc.

Heading off to meet Fred, I'm wearing some of Oliver's old clothes—jeans with pockets like diagonal slashes, a jumper that's the color of eggplant, and a big gray jacket that Oliver tells me is made from boiled wool, by some Japanese designer. It all looks a bit weird to me, but I decide the trend guru knows more than the dag guru about what to wear.

Fred walks a full circle around me.

"You look older, taller, and cooler. How's that possible in a couple of weeks?"

"I'm running every day, with Howard, and pumping the doorstops."

"I see the results. You'll lose that whole geeky charm thing you've got happening if you're not careful."

I give him a good solid punch in the arm.

"Hey, I might have a girl for you," I say. "She's in my class, and she's maybe going to be looking for someone to ask to the social soon."

"What's wrong with her?" Fred asks.

"That's a low-self-esteem question, my friend," I say.

"Does she have pimples? Is that why she'd go with me?"

"A few pimples. But she's pretty, and smart, and nice. And she's got a sense of humor. I don't even know if she'd take you, but I'm planning to suggest it—if you're okay with that?"

He's unconvinced—extremely choosy for someone with no track record with girls at all.

"I'll think about it. Will you be asking the unattainable one?"

I let out a deep sigh. "I don't think I've got the guts anyway, but I'll never find out because I'm pretty sure she's asking someone else."

We're in the queue for movie tickets. Fred gets out his wallet.

"Plan B says pay for your ticket, because of the crisis. She said no arguments. Is it still on?"

"Worse than ever. She's still talking people out of getting married, but I don't want you to pay."

"What part of 'no arguments' don't you understand?"

"I feel bad."

"Would you do the same for me?"

"Of course."

"Then shut up about it. Your problems are my problems."

"I'm making some money, though, but I feel like I need to save it for emergencies."

"Yeah, you should. I'm not being nice, Dan. And it's not even my money. But the person who's got more should pay more, it's only fair. Think of it in political terms."

"Okay, but only if I keep a record, and then I pay you back when the crisis is over. Or buy you the same amount of movie tickets, or whatever."

"Not necessary. But if that's what it takes, fine."

The movie's not much good, after all that. I zone out and start thinking about work this morning. I did the early shift and so did Janie. She was no friendlier to me than usual. Which you'd think she would be if she wants to soften me up for this big ask, whatever it might turn out to be. Unless she thought she was being nice when she told me on our break, "Forget Estelle; everybody loves her, and you don't even rate."

After the movie, Fred and I go our separate ways. He's got homework. We don't get homework. But I've got motherwork. I figure if I can't manage to be properly nice to her, I can at least dig up someone who can be.

She's in a good mood when I get back. Radiohead is blaring at high volume, and there's some cash sitting on the kitchen table. Mrs. Da Silva has picked up the cake.

"A paying customer. A satisfied, paying customer. We should celebrate. How about takeaway for dinner?" she says.

"Can we afford it?"

"Not really, but, hey, we could all be dead tomorrow. Let's live it up."

That's her version of a cheery comment at the moment.

"Okay."

My plan is to ring my mother's friend Rachel. I ask her to come around and to invite their other friend, Alice, as a surprise for my mother. I suggest they might like to bring takeaway. More shameless sponging.

"I don't know, Dan," she says. "I've tried to catch up more than once, but I'm still getting the same, very clear *stay away* message. I think she wants to settle in alone for a while."

"She might say that, but it's not what she needs. She's gone all weird about Thom Yorke."

There's a pause.

"It happened with Bono, the year after we left school," says Rachel. "Your dad led a house intervention to confiscate and destroy *The Joshua Tree*. I still can't listen to it to this day."

"She's by herself too much. The business is going really badly. She never goes out anywhere, and she probably needs someone to talk to besides me."

It's a massive relief to blurt it all out.

"Okay, honey, I'll call Alice. We'll come early with food. I won't call and let her put me off."

Rachel is my godmother and my mother's oldest friend. They shared a house with my dad and Alice when they were at university. Alice is a very brainy journalist. Rachel is a legal aid lawyer who, my mother says, has "no illusions" about some of her clients. That means quite a few of them are crooks, but they need representation just like the innocent ones.

Seeing her friends seems to cheer her up, although she cries and hugs them when they come in bearing food and wine, and says, "I look like a mess."

To which Alice says, "It suits you."

We go into the formal dining room to eat. Lebanese food; it's great. They have a couple of glasses of wine each, and they're off, all talking at the top of their voices. I leave them to it. Or pretend to. I stay outside the door and listen. How else am I going to find stuff out?

"The problem was we kept trading after Rob knew things were down the gurgler. Not that *I* knew at the time. I think he was hoping for a last-minute miracle."

"It's a shame after all the hard slog," says Alice.

"You could have told us about the big gay scandal sooner, lovey," says Rachel.

"You were the first to hear. After me," says my mother.

"Remember we all thought he was gay when we first met him?" says Alice. "Too handsome to be straight, we thought."

"We were right," says my mother, and they laugh like lunatics.

"Be fair, though, he gave it a pretty good go," says Rachel. "Baby and everything."

"I'm bereft, of course," says my mother. "But I'll get there. I'm sure I'll be happy for him one of these days. Possibly after I get some post-breakup sex." They all laugh again. I really shouldn't be hearing this.

"He couldn't have come out way back then, anyway, even if he knew," says Alice. "Remember his family? Those awful parents!"

"My hideous in-laws. May they rest in peace. No, they would have had him executed or something. It took him all this time..."

"Didn't he used to say he was bisexual way back then?" asks Rachel.

"It was probably as close as he could come to saying 'I'm gay.' If I wasn't so dim, I might have picked up on it," says my mother.

"We were babies. What did we know?" says Rachel.

"No, she's right," says Alice. "He was your best friend, you slept with him, got yourself knocked up, and forced him to live a lie!" More laughing.

"But all these years, you were still...?"

"Not so much."

Aaaagh! Too much information.

I lean back and look up at the hallway ceiling. Crazed and stained. The ceiling, not me. Sounds like my dad tried to be as honest as he could be back in the day. My grandparents sound dodgy. If your own parents won't let you be who you are, who will?

"Dan's been amazing," I hear, with amazement. "He's got a job, settled into his school. He's really risen to the challenge. Hardly complained at all." I'm burning with shame when I hear this. A generous interpretation, I'd call it. Listening to how good I've been makes me feel like the lowest of the low. She doesn't mention the cold war, or my pissy behavior about her scaring off clients. Is it loyalty? Does she really not notice that stuff? Or does she suspect I'm listening at the door?

"Rob must be missing him."

"Horribly. Dan doesn't want to speak to him yet, though."

"Well, he has walked out on the kid," says Alice.

"He'd be just as happy for Dan to live with him, but we thought it'd be better if he stays with me. At least I know we can settle here. Thank you, Adelaide! What I would have done without this place, I don't know."

"We'd have taken you in," says Rachel.

"Speak for yourself," says Alice.

"Rob would be around here in a second, if Dan would see him. Of course *I* don't want to see him for a while."

"He's a proper bastard!" says Alice.

"Bastard!" agrees Rachel.

I'd like to find out more about how he stuffed up the family business and sent us bankrupt, but it's not like I can slip an eavesdropper request under the door.

"And why couldn't he have gone ten years ago when I was still good-looking?" my mother says. "What hope have I got now?" And they're laughing again. It must be the wine.

I casually return for some baklava, and disappear again when they start asking me about girls.

As I leave, Alice proposes a toast to Rob, and, in memory of his "interminable" lists, they launch into the "top ten bastards we're better off without" list, to more gales of laughter.

But I'm thinking he's maybe less of a bastard than I thought.

19

My mother's in a good mood and seems relaxed for the first time in ages. She thanks me for asking Rachel and Alice over.

It's Monday, and my fifteenth birthday.

Big deal.

We have pancakes for breakfast, with lots of sugar and lemon juice—the best way. My present is a small stuffed crocodile with green glass eyes—a bit morbid, perhaps, but I love it. And Rachel left a present when she came for dinner; it's the same every year, books. This year it's *Catch-22*, by Joseph Heller, a self-help book for boys living without fathers, and *The Right Stuff*, by Tom Wolfe.

My dad calls while we're having breakfast. "He's here,"

my mother says, nodding coercively as she hands me the phone. "It's Rob." She has the mouthpiece covered.

"I'm not here," I say.

"Just say hello," she says. So, only because I think it will make her feel better, I take the phone.

His voice spills with emotion, and hearing him smile makes me want to cry—go figure—which I would rather cut off my head than do. With a lump the size of an apple in my throat, it's as short a conversation as I can manage. He says, "Happy Birthday, Dan." I say, "Thanks." He says, "How are you?" I say, "Fine." He reminds me of the present he's left for me. I say, "Okay. Bye," and hang up.

It's hard to believe my mother when she tells me it won't always be this hard. I honestly can't see how it's going to change.

Even at school I can't get my father out of my head. Pittney is late for homeroom and there's some feral stuff happening. One of the homie boys is off his meds and roving around tagging people's books. Mel, a transposable parenthesis, says he can tag her, and offers the inside of her thigh, on which he writes his phone number. Jayzo is leaning on one of his friends to lend him money. Estelle, Uyen, and Janie are talking together. I sit nearby, and they start talking to me, which draws the attention of Jayzo and Deeks.

"Why would you talk to the cake boy?" ask Jayzo.

"Why would you care?" says Estelle.

"I don't," he says. Then proves he does by hanging around, needling and abusing us. It makes it kind of hard to concentrate. We try ignoring him, but he doesn't like that. He craves attention like a two-year-old. He grabs Janie's phone. It's her favorite thing; she's always making little videos on it. And I know she doesn't have much spare money, so if it gets broken it's a big deal. She goes to grab it back, but he chucks it to Deeks. There's no point chasing the phone, it'll just get thrown around some more.

"Give it back," I hear myself saying.

"What's that?" says Jayzo.

"Cake boy's talking tough," says Deeks.

"Give her phone back," I say.

"Make me," says Jayzo.

Is there anything more pathetic yet frustratingly effective that someone bigger and stronger can say?

No one's expecting me to do anything. No one is ever stupid enough to take on Jayzo. Deeks is just standing there, holding the phone out of reach and grinning like a chimp. I feel all my anger dots join up in a surge of really hating Jayzo's stupid bullying and intimidation. The element of surprise is on my side and I use it. I grab Deeks's wrist hard, take the phone, and hand it back to Janie. Deeks is wincing and grimacing as though I've really hurt him. Good. I hope I have.

"You faggot," Deeks says.

With a wash of relief I realize that, even though I can't talk to him, I'm on my dad's side. I feel angry on his behalf.

I want to defend him. I hate that these idiots use "faggot" and "gay" as insults. And they do it all the time.

"Stop using that as a put-down. There's nothing wrong with people being gay. And don't use 'girl' as an insult, either. Half the people in this room are girls."

Jayzo looks stunned and says, "Yeah, well, that's what I'd expect from a...gay...girl." He is, for this one glorious moment, completely deflated.

It feels great not letting myself be intimidated by someone I despise.

"Slam dunk," says Lou.

"Mmm, thanks," says Janie grudgingly.

I stop lying low in class and instead recklessly expose myself as the nerd I am. Forget "under the radar." I answer questions like there's no tomorrow.

As Lou correctly points out, there may well be no tomorrow for me, if Jayzo gets me alone on the way home.

"I don't care," I say. "At least he'll know I'm his intellectual superior."

That cracks her up.

"You assume he can draw conclusions. He's barely smart enough to draw breath."

At lunchtime, Jayzo hangs around near Estelle, Janie, and Uyen. It makes me edgy.

"Probably apologizing for acting like a sexist, homophobic thug," I say.

"More likely sniffing around to see if he can get Estelle to go to the social with him," says Lou.

I snort with laughter at the very idea.

"They went out last year," she says. "Year-eight relationship, so it lasted about five minutes, but still..."

How can that be true? The picture of perfection and the missing link?

Lou follows my look of incredulity.

"He's pretty good-looking, you know," she says. "And he reformed briefly; they put him on a good behavior contract. Given up on him now, of course."

I remember Fred.

"I've got a friend you can ask, if you're not already taking someone," I say.

Her look is hard to read. It's certainly not "thrilled" or "delighted."

"What's wrong with him?" she asks. "Has he got pimples? Is that it? No girlfriend? No one else wants him?"

Lou and Fred are so perfect for each other it makes me want to dance.

"I'll let you know closer to the time," she says. "I'll have a better sense of (a) if I'm going and (b) if so, how desperate I am."

"She couldn't possibly say yes, could she?" Lou follows my eye line back to Estelle.

"I don't know, Dan," she says, with a small sigh.

Estelle walks with me as far as Phrenology. We don't talk. She's listening to Kings of Leon with one ear. I suspect she's trying to protect me from Jayzo while he cools down, maybe thinking he's less likely to thump me if she's there. I hope she's right.

"I like their early stuff much better," I say.

"Me too," she says.

As she's about to walk off, putting the second earbud in, she smiles and says, "Thanks for today."

20

So the question is why, just when I've had the smallest of breakthroughs with Estelle, do I decide to risk a third visit to the attic?

There are two reasons. I need to find out what they were talking about in the garden. It's eating me up. And I somehow brought an earring back on my jumper sleeve on my last visit, which I need to return.

It's why I've been sitting here waiting between the heavy and the sheer curtains in the front sitting room's bay window looking out onto the street. The minutes drag; I would never have the patience to work as a private investigator. I'm watching for something I know happens at this time, and here it is. Estelle is walking out her front door, turning right, and heading up the hill wheeling her cello case. I have a clear hour, minimum.

The books are still off the hatch when I climb up into that other world. I have a delayed lightbulb. Having now seen Estelle's modern interior, I realize she must have built her nest with stuff from Adelaide's side of the attic. Welcome to my world of crime.

I flick the flashlight around and open the lid of a wooden trunk. It's full of folded clothes. As I rummage, a smell of spice wafts up. I pull out a pile of long, collarless men's shirts, no buttons, pleated fronts, and a couple of women's dresses made from sheer material with tiny beads sewn into it. They're all wrapped in tissue paper. Who wrapped them? When did they expect to use them again?

Another trunk is full of silky fabrics—it's been rifled through for sure. This is the stuff Estelle has pinned to the walls. Beside the trunk is a huge leather suitcase, now home to woolen and mohair blankets. Whoever stored them has carefully placed lavender between each layer, so long ago now the lavender disintegrates between my fingers. All this stuff belonging to lives no longer being lived. You really don't want to think too much about it.

I open one more trunk, this one covered in cracked black leather, with dull brass clasps and pasted-on destination labels. There's a huge dead animal inside. I jump back, yelping with fright—an embarrassing noise in hindsight— as I see that of course it's fur coats, not a corpse. The stink that rises from them is the ghost of mothballs, not rotting flesh.

Pushing the packing cases aside for the third time, I once again feel an overpowering surge of conscience, and, once again, I put it aside.

Hardened spy that I am, I first place the returned earring carefully under the desk, then go straight to the most recent diary volume and scan. There's an entry about a film Janie's making. That must be what they needed a murderer for. I obviously didn't make the cut. I read on. Bad news. There's someone Estelle likes now. She calls him disc boy. Fortunate disc boy:

He's cute because he doesn't have a clue he is. His
hair is long and floppy, and when he's concentrating
it goes into his eyes and he does an impatient
backward flick of his head. He looks like he's in
another space.

This must be the guy she's taking to the social. A quick scan of our class, hmm, the description could possibly fit one or two unworthies. More likely someone from year ten. I feel sick thinking about it.

The most superficial punishment for the snooper is to discover something you don't want to know. The real punishment is living with what you've done. I'm getting the double whammy.

I put the notebook back and look around. Whoa! How did I not notice that?

Estelle has put up a whole lot of photographs where one of the silk hangings was. There are twenty: five rows of four. Pictures of the sky taken from the same window, its frame framing the images. Each one is beautiful in itself but the picture they make together knocks me out. It's about how things can be the same but so utterly different. It's my life—my father is still my father, only he's gay and gone. My mother is the same, only she's happy about ninety percent less than she used to be. I'm the same, only I hardly remember who I used to be. Especially my heart, which now has parts I didn't even know existed before.

I step back to get the impact of the overall pattern of skies—and being so engrossed is perhaps why I don't realize the trapdoor cover is lifting. But I spin around fast enough when I hear Estelle's astonished gasp.

In her fright at seeing me, she sways slightly. Worried she might fall, I step across the space, steady her shoulders, and give her a hand up. We stand, face-to-face.

Is she as affected by our closeness as I am? She's wet; tiny droplets cling to the edges of her hair. And the rain now hammering onto the slates above us is just a faint echo of the blood beating through my veins. She smells like damp sweater and flowers. I have no idea what to do next, but she does. She grabs her hand back, her clear eyes glinting.

"Wh-what are you doing here?" I manage to say.

"What am *I* doing here? *Me*? In *my* own attic?"

"I just...don't you have a cello lesson?"

Big mistake.

"Canceled. How do you even know I do cello? Are you spying on me? Are you a stalker or something?"

"No!" Not technically. "I've noticed this is the time you take your cello for a walk. Is that a crime?"

"Is this the first time you've been here?" Her eyes go straight to the diaries—which look completely undisturbed.

"Yes! I heard a noise...a few minutes ago."

Lies, more lies.

"What sort of noise?"

"Like a bang. I just wanted to see what it was."

I think she's buying it.

"You better not have touched any of my stuff!"

"No. I...as if...I...of course not," I say, mustering an indignant tone from somewhere. "I haven't touched a thing." A confession right now would only lead to violence. "I just found it...by accident...That's my attic, there," I say, pointing to the hole in our shared wall.

"Exactly. Your attic." She points. "My attic." She points again.

"I'd say you're welcome to visit my attic anytime, but I guess you've already been," I say.

She has the grace to look self-conscious, remembering all the loot she has taken from Adelaide's side.

"I figured no one was using it. Take it back, if you want."

"It might as well be used," I say, turning to go.

"You can't tell anyone about this place. My parents don't know I come up here. Nobody knows."

"They must know they've got an attic."

"They're not 'spare junk' people. They forget it's even here. Promise you won't tell."

"I won't."

"Promise."

"I promise."

"For whatever it's worth, I was beginning to think you were someone I could...trust—someone with a bit of backbone."

"You can trust me."

"Not after this. I feel all snooped on. We're back to square one, as far as I'm concerned."

"I had to find out. It's been killing me since I heard them talking," I tell Howard. "Don't you understand? They were talking about *me*. I had a right to know what it was about."

He's unconvinced.

So am I.

"Square one! I've really blown it. What am I going to do now?"

Howard sighs and resettles, chin on paw, looking at me. It's the psychotherapist look again: You figure it out.

"Come on, let's go for a run. It might do your limp some good to have a bit of exercise."

He gets up very slowly, stretching out first one then the other back leg with little creaky shudders.

The next time Janie and I are on a work break together, she straightaway asks, "What did you do to get Stell so mad?"

"What did she tell you?"

"That you weren't as nice as you seemed. That it was just as well we didn't ask you to be in the film."

"What film?"

That's correct: Lies and deception lead to further lies and deception.

"My film. We thought you could be the guy who kills the main character, but then we decided not to use humans..."

Interesting... Estelle hasn't told Janie about the attic. It means that, despite what she said, she must at least trust me enough to keep her secret. It's a crumb, but it's all I've got.

Anne comes out with semolina cakes for us, the ones with a smooth almond pressed into the middle of the diamond. She tells us to eat them up and head back inside, it's getting busy.

Over the next couple of weeks, school comes down to a few activities: trying to find time alone with Estelle to make amends, trying to avoid being alone with Jayzo, and trying to get Lou to agree to meet Fred.

At home I monitor my mother, avoid my father's calls, pick up and put down the unopened present from him no more than three or four times a day, run every night, and lift the weights with increasing ease. The muscles are starting to appear, and seeing that feels better than it should. Hello, guns.

Finally, it's getting a bit warmer. It's spring in a few weeks, and occasionally the mornings aren't quite so freezing. I've set up the former maid's bedroom as a television room, with a heater. So between that and the kitchen, and either being in a hot bath or in bed with a hot water bottle, the house is physically more bearable than I would have thought possible when we first moved in.

It's Pittney who finally gives me time alone with Estelle. She and I both go to pick up the last class copy of *Math Alive* at the same time. I had it first, so I hold on to it. She glares at me, and holds on, too. She gives the book a tug. That offends my sense of fair play, so I tug back. With devious timing she lets go and I go flying, landing in Jayzo's lap. He gives me an almighty shove, which sends me colliding into Estelle, who falls on the floor and says with heavy sarcasm as I help her up, "Thanks, Dan."

With his own brand of oblivious logic, Pittney says, "Right, that's it. I've had enough of you three. See me after class."

That's how the three of us end up being the year-nine spring social steering committee.

None of us wants the job.

Jayzo spends the first meeting trying to get Estelle to go with him to the social. He's too thick to realize it's not going to happen. I finally can't take it anymore. "She said no, just leave her alone and ask someone else."

Instead of being grateful, Estelle turns on me. "Who asked you to speak for me?"

"Yeah, just leave her alone," Jayzo says with moronic delight.

I've had enough of both of them.

"Pittney said we have to put something on paper before we leave. And I've got to get to work. What's our theme? Anyone got any bright ideas?" I say.

Estelle flips through a book Pittney has left for us, and reads out some pathetic suggestions: "Then and Now, Circus, Happily Ever After, Freaks and Geeks..."

Jayzo likes Rubik's Cube, because it involves people taking their clothes off.

We end up settling on the most obvious idea: Black Tie. So we'll be having a formal social, which sounds stupid. Perfect. Because it will be. I write it on a bit of paper and we leave.

On the way out, Jayzo stops me, blocking my path. "Cake boy, how'd you like some squashed eyeballs spread on maggoty scabs?" He then does an excellent impression of someone about to vomit. I'm unprepared, and it works. The familiar light-headed feeling washes over me. I feel cold, then really hot. Just before I black out, Estelle shoves me into a chair and pushes my head in the direction of the floor.

"Leave the wuss alone, you thug," she says.

Jayzo leaves, smirking.

"Who asked you to speak for me?" I can't resist saying.

"If I hadn't you would've fainted again. Then I'd just waste more time looking for a teacher."

Fair point.

Janie and Uyen are outside waiting for Estelle. Again I relegate myself to the other side of the road as they walk toward the shops, yakking their heads off, occasionally looking over toward me. Are they hoping I'll go away? Are they worried I can overhear? I go into the thrift store, and see Estelle heading up to the Arts Project space.

Mrs. Nelson doesn't look exactly thrilled to see me. But then, she never does. I try not to feel sensitive about it. I haven't broken anything since that first day.

She asks me to tidy the magazines. This is the same job I did last time, and the time before that. It's not that they aren't messy, they are, but do they really need me here? The book and magazine corner is like a library to some of our customers. We sell furniture as well as clothes and house junk, and people often just settle on a sofa, a kitchen chair, or a stool and hunker down for an hour or so of browsing. Sometimes Mrs. Nelson makes cups of tea for everyone and they all talk about celebrity news. The magazines are old and shuffled, and although the lack of chronology causes some confused arguments, it doesn't spoil anyone's fun; it just adds to the sense of celebrities living in their own mad world.

It's way past time to bite the bullet. "Do you need me here, Mrs. Nelson?"

"We value your contribution, Dan. There's no question of that."

"But do you really *need* me?"

"I want you to know you are always needed here. You're reliable and generous with your time, and we certainly appreciate you."

I try another tack. "If I could get more paid work, would it be a problem if I couldn't come here anymore?"

She beams, finally getting my drift.

"Not at all! Not in the slightest. I've got more volunteers than I can poke a stick at."

She might have let on a bit earlier.

I go straight over the road to Phrenology. Ali says he can give me one more after-school shift, but he's in one of his moods, so I head for the kitchen to get out of his way.

Anne is in there, looking grim. She cuts fiercely into a slab of still-warm poppyseed slice, handing me a piece. A vat of soup that smells like tomato and cumin is bubbling away. She nods at the pot. "Give that a stir, will you, Dan? Make sure the lentils aren't sticking." I pick up a big wooden spoon and stir.

"What's up?"

"I just reminded Ali that I'm going on my holiday with

Irena. I told him a hundred times we're going, but he never believed it."

"Where are you going?"

"A gourmet tour of Southeast Asia with Tony Tan. A tour of Loire region chateaux, and then on to Florence, to stay with Irena's sister."

"When?"

"Next week."

"How long are you away?"

"Eight weeks. I told him months ago. Has he planned for it? No!"

I go out the back way. No point getting in the line of fire.

Mrs. Da Silva has a bag of scraps for Howard when I drop in on the way home. I tell her the Phrenology news.

"What will you do with your extra money?"

"Take Howard to the vet. His limp isn't getting any better."

"No surprise there. All those long runs, Dan. He's a very old dog."

"He never used to limp."

"And I never used to have bunions. Mind the shop for a minute?"

I stand behind the counter and she disappears out the back into the house. I imagine Phrenology without Anne. Who's going to do all the cooking? What if they get someone who's no good? And they lose customers. And the business goes down the tube. And my job disappears. A brilliant idea strikes as I sell a kid some bread. My mother's a fantastic cook. God knows she's got time on her hands. Why shouldn't she fill in for Anne? She needs to get out more, spend less time alone with Thom Yorke...Perfect.

Mrs. Da Silva comes out a couple of minutes later with some plastic food containers. Full.

"I made curries this morning. Take some home."

"Thanks. What do you think about my mum filling in for Anne?"

She smiles. "You're not just a pretty face."

21

Coming through the back gate, I almost run into Oliver.

"Score," he says, when he sees the food.

"Come and eat with us? There's heaps."

"Great. I need to talk to you about something, too. Seven-ish?"

When I open the kitchen door my mother is singing along with Thom. I hate to intrude, but I try to sell her on the idea of running the Phrenology kitchen while I help with the rice and dahl and a salad. "It's a couple of cakes and biscuits each day, and stuff like soup, some pides, and frittata for the lunches, and that's it. No dinners. You could do it with your eyes shut."

"Who's going to look after my business?"

"Let the answering machine worry about it. If you get an order, you can fit it in. I'll help. It's not like you're batting clients off with a stick."

Privately, I'm thinking that's exactly what it's like, just not in the commonly understood meaning of the phrase.

Oliver brings over hot, garlicky naan from the take-away and some cold beer, and tries to help me persuade my mother to go for the Phrenology job. "You're alone too much. It's bad for your brain-health," he says. Let's hope this sinks in.

The thing he wants to talk to me about is work-related, too. He's going to London for a couple of weeks for work, then coming back with his girlfriend, and he wants me to look after his place.

Am I interested in the job? Only utterly and absolutely. A world where I get paid to sit around in the best place I know, switch lights and music on and off (so it looks inhabited), and collect the mail seems too good to be true.

Back at school, Pittney's starting to crack it about the social arrangements. He tells us part of our task is "canvassing the views" of our classmates. Does he have even half a clue about the impossible contradictions this throws up?

"Socials are stupid, I'm not coming."

"Get my brother's band or I'm not coming."

"I'm not coming if I have to wear a suit."

"I'm not coming unless people are totally dressing up."

"It has to be dance music or no one will dance."

"If it's just dance music I'm not coming."

"There better be good food for twenty bucks or it's a total rip-off."

"There better not be food or it'll just turn into a food fight."

"There better be no teachers inside or I'm not coming."

"You need security and door checks or people are just going to get trashed, and if anyone pukes on my new dress, they are dead."

"What kind of loser would spend a Friday night at a lame school dance?"

All the canvassing does is make us realize that no matter what we decide, some people are going to hate the social and probably hate us, too. Once we cover the event insurance and security, and throw around a bit of decoration, there's not going to be much money left over for food and music. We don't know how much exactly until we start selling tickets, so we put that job on the top of the list.

"We'd better book Vile Bodies, too," Estelle says.

Jayzo nods.

"Who?" I ask.

"The band, jerk-off."

"I don't even know them."

"Now, food..." Estelle's acting like the band is a done deal.

"Wait up, what kind of music do they do?"

"They're good. They do their own stuff and okay covers."

"What about all the people who only want dance music?" I say.

"Tough," says Jayzo.

"But why don't we get a DJ? Then they can play different music and cover a few more bases."

"Let's vote," says Estelle, getting annoyed. "Two against one. Now can we move on?"

I'm getting annoyed, too. "That's a completely half-arsed way to figure this out," I persist.

"What have you got against democracy?" she wants to know.

"Nothing, but you're not exactly representing your constituents, if you want to get technical." I look at my list of "canvassed" opinions. "At least half want electronic dance stuff."

"The band is available, reliable, affordable, and good," she says. She's not budging, and Jayzo's on her side. So why do I care? I'm not even planning to go. I've got an overdeveloped sense of trying to do the job we've been given. I shelve it. Who cares?

"Fine," I say. "Let's have pathetic Muse covers and no one dancing all night. It'll be great."

"Fine! We'll play Daft Punk in the break. Happy?"

"Ecstatic."

Estelle and I head to reading group.

"You got here five minute ago," she says. "Why do you think you've got a clue?"

"I didn't ask for this job," I remind her.

"Me neither. And it's your fault I've got it!"

That's rich. She really did grab that book after I picked it up.

"Try your fault."

"Huh! Typical!"

"You wouldn't know what's typical for me."

"I know all I need to know." She says it as though she's written me off.

"You don't know anything about me."

"I know you had me under surveillance. Then coincidentally you turn up in my attic."

"It *was* a coincidence." I sound so plausibly indignant. "And it was mean to say what you said to Janie. I didn't blab to her about your attic room."

"Keep up the good work and you'll be human one of these days."

>> <<

During reading group Estelle and Janie are hatching something. Even with my healthy level of paranoia, I can tell they're not talking about me. But something's up. I hear a couple of phrases floating into the ether, "only chance," "underage," "they never check."

Lou pokes me in the ribs. "Pay attention, will you? You're distracting me."

"Do you know what they're talking about?"

"Don't know, don't care. Hey, I'll meet your friend."

"Great."

"Don't get all excited. I'm only doing it out of self-defense. My mother heard about the social and she's trying to set me up with some loser son of a friend of hers. What's his name again?"

"Fred."

Lou looks at me looking at Estelle with a mixture of pity and irritation.

"Why don't you just ask her, for god's sake?"

"Who?"

"Estelle, dummy. She can only say no."

"That's what she'd definitely say, so why bother?"

"Because maybe then you can stop obsessing about her."

"I'm not obsessing," I say.

She rolls her eyes. "And I don't have pimples." Like Fred, she can read me like a book.

"Anyway, I'm not planning on going."

"Yeah, you're going. You're on the committee. You're setting me up with your friend. So, jeez, you're in it up to your elbows."

After school, I take Howard to the vet. I've got sixty bucks and I figure that should just about cover the bill. Wrong. I come out with two types of bad news and a hundred-dollar deficit.

The vet examined and X-rayed Howard, and found he has a ruptured cruciate ligament in his back leg and pretty bad arthritis. The prognosis is awful. Pain will increase. Mobility will decrease. Medication might help, but a year's supply is more than a thousand dollars. An operation where they put in a prosthetic tendon might help. That would cost at least fifteen hundred dollars, and there's no guarantee it'll even work.

The vet suggested that given Howard's age, things might get to the point where I have to consider putting him down. But she said "euthanize" him, as though that makes it any better. Howard's not getting any younger, I'm not getting any richer, and I have no idea what I should do.

By the time we get home I'm crying. Howard is so waggy, limping along beside me, tail up in the air. It's just unbearable. It's as though he's saying, I love walking with you, Dan. There's nowhere else I'd rather be.

Or maybe he's just saying he opposes euthanasia. Which you would, in the circumstances.

Estelle is arriving home. She waits till we get to our gate. I have time to sniff and wipe my face. I'm pretty sure she can't see I've been crying.

"Hey," she says.

"Hi," I croak back.

"What's up?"

"Nothing—it's just Howard's sick."

"What's wrong with him?"

"It's his leg." I'm too choked up to explain it.

"Vets can do anything these days. There's even chemotherapy for dogs."

Exactly what I would have thought back in the land of money.

She leans in and gives me a quick kiss on the cheek. It's over before I've even registered it's happening.

"Does that mean I'm forgiven?"

"Not even close." But she turns back to me as she reaches her front door. "Don't worry, they'll fix him up." And she's gone.

I take Howard inside, realizing that the kiss bears no resemblance to an actual kiss. Those girls are always giving each other kisses and hugs. Even so, yesterday it would have made me feel a lot better than it does now, weighed down as I am by the understanding that I live in a household where expensive vet treatments are as impossible as Estelle kissing me like she means it.

Howard deserves an extra ear rub and tummy scratch and he gets them. I can't work out a solution to the problem. I've got enough saved to pay the hundred dollars I owe, but that wipes out the puny nest-egg fund. I could cover the medication, so long as I keep my shifts up. But the operation's out of reach. There's no way I can put that much money together.

I feel a useless aching wash of anger and sadness that my father isn't here to fix things. I can't figure this out on my own.

I've tried to jam memories of him in a box I don't open. But I let myself have a dip in now. I imagine we're having a guy night. Sometimes when my mother went to Thursday night Pilates class and then to dinner with the Pilates women, we used to make a deliberately unhealthy meal together, the sort she'd never eat. My dad used to say, "It's our duty, Dan. We're providing balance in the universe."

We'd go shopping and get some kransky sausages—they're really fatty and cheesy. We'd get onions and potatoes and cook up a massive batch of fried onions and chips and have two or three hot dogs each, with pickles and mustard and sauce. Strictly no green vegetables or salad allowed. We'd drink Coke and do huge, loud burps, like we never did around her. Then we'd clean up, air out the kitchen, get rid of all the evidence, and watch a DVD together, something with good fights and car chases, the kind she hates.

On this sort of night I could ask my dad, "What are we going to do about Howard?" and he'd say, "Sounds like he needs that operation. Leave it with me." Problems were solved as easily as that. It's like remembering a fairy tale, or remembering a time I believed in fairy tales. I had no idea how easy life was.

Letting myself remember these things makes me feel

worse. The closed-box policy is a good one. I still hurt. No less than when he left.

And I'm crying again. This can't be healthy. I'm drowning. Everything feels so relentless and impossible. It's like trying to run with no traction. There's no one to depend on, no one solving problems, no one picking up the tab, no one to pass the buck to. There's just me, with no money, and no solutions—and my mother, with a failing business, a Thom Yorke obsession, and a need to be protected from any more bad news.

>> <<

There's oatmeal on the stove in the morning. And the smell of cinnamon. A cooked breakfast is usually a sign of a positive frame of mind. My mother is sitting with the bills folder open in front of her.

"Dan, I have no choice. I'm applying for the job at Phrenology."

"Fantastic." I wonder if this means there's a chance for Howard's operation. But it's short-lived.

"I'm on final reminders for half of these. I just can't pay them. And the bank's not going to keep coming to the party unless I can rustle up a bit of income."

"Do you want me to tell Ali?"

"No, thanks, sweetie. I'll go and see him today."

She looks resigned rather than happy, but at least she's going to apply. I hope Ali hasn't found anyone in the meantime.

Estelle comes out of her gate as I leave, and we walk to school together. Why the sudden comradeship? I'm suspicious. Maybe she did notice I was crying yesterday and has decided I'm a pathetic charity case. I can live with that.

Walking along beside her all I can think is lucky old disc boy, with his damn flippy hair.

"Are you angry?" Estelle asks.

"Me? No. Why?"

"You look really angry."

"Just—thoughtful."

I keep stacking on these desirable attributes. Fainter. Stalker. Tearful. Thoughtful. Disc boy's list probably runs more along the lines of athletic, sexy, good sense of humor. I've got a good sense of humor. Why can't I think of something funny to say?

We stomp on in thoughtful silence.

When we get to school, she fixes me with a pointed look and says, "Maybe I have been too quick to judge you, Dan."

"R-right." What's this about?

"So, how would you like another chance?"

"Sure." I'm hardly going to say no to a death row reprieve.

"Home economics room at recess. We have a proposition for you."

"Okay."

There's no point in pretending I can concentrate on earth sciences. I'm burning with curiosity and anxiety. Is the film back on the drawing board? I can't act to save my life. But I'll try anything if it means time with Estelle.

The home economics room has its own smell of rancid butter and cheap spray-on bench cleaner. They're waiting for me.

"First up, you are sworn to secrecy, whether or not you agree to be part of this."

Fair enough, commercial-in-confidence, creative privilege and all that.

"Okay, yeah."

"Well, swear then."

"I swear I won't tell anyone about...?"

"What you're about to hear."

"What I'm about to hear," I say, looking from one face to the other.

They look at each other, agreeing to go ahead.

"You'd better sit down."

"Janie put her film in a competition."

"*Hanging on the Telephone.* Short crime narratives you download on your phone."

"And she found out on Tuesday she's one of ten finalists."

"Congratulations." So far, I can't see where I come into this.

"I get to go to Sydney for the announcement of the winner."

The girls look at each other.

"That's where we have a couple of teeny little hitches."

"How teeny?" I ask, becoming suspicious.

"Janie used her fake ID to enter. You had to be eighteen or over."

"And I have to go to Sydney, but I can't tell my parents. No way they'd let me."

"So, what are you going to do?"

"We pooled our money to get the bus ticket."

"And we've told my parents that I'm staying over at Estelle's."

"We do it all the time."

"They never check up on us."

"The bus leaves at five thirty tomorrow morning," says Estelle.

"Then I go to the awards and screening, and I'm back on the overnighter to Melbourne."

"So Janie will come back to my place. My parents are never home when I get home from school."

"Then, Estelle's got this attic..."

Estelle looks at me. Our secret. She hasn't told Janie about my trespass.

"Janie's going to hide up there, get up at five, and go to the bus depot."

"Only..." They look at each other again. This is obviously where I come into it.

"My mother's an incredibly light sleeper and downstairs

is all alarmed at night. And the alarm shows a record of when it's switched off and on . . ." begins Estelle.

"So Estelle thinks we can get out through your attic. She says there's a tree that just about touches the back of your house. I could climb down that."

"No," I say.

22

With Oliver's key in my pocket, I've got a better plan. I suggest Janie hides out at Oliver's until it's time to go, Estelle comes out via my attic to avoid her security alarm, and I go with them to the bus depot.

"We don't need you to come," says Janie.

"What if you get harassed by a carload of random thugs?"

"We won't," says Estelle.

But they end up agreeing that it's not a bad idea to have a tall male and a loud dog in tow wandering the streets in the pitch-black early hours.

As I go over the plan with them it strikes me as dangerous, illegal, crazy, and bound to fail.

It seems risky to assume that just because their parents never *have* called about sleepover arrangements, they never *will* call. And Janie looks her age—fifteen with too much makeup—so won't it be obvious to the people running the competition that she's faked her ID? That'll blow things out of the water, for sure. And I'm not even half convinced that it's safe for her to be in Sydney all by herself with nothing on her but a fake ID. What if something happens to her? No one will even know who she is.

They think I'm worrying about nothing and I have to hand it to them, they've done their homework. They're usually not allowed to have school night sleepovers, but Janie has been laying the groundwork about the demands of our earth sciences project, so she has permission for a Thursday and Friday night sleepover. They've timed the walk to the bus depot: twenty minutes exactly. They're packing Janie's lunch and snacks, and she has a ten-dollar allocation for a takeaway dinner.

Estelle's mother is in the middle of preparing a catalog for some exhibition of Asian artifacts. Estelle knows this is a reliably vague and distracted time for her.

We're still fine-tuning the plan when I realize I haven't even seen the film. So they show me. It's a murder mystery. They've used stop-motion photography with three Barbies and a Ken doll. There are also two Power Rangers in the cast with the disconcerting ability to flip their heads around one-eighty degrees to display either a face or a mask. The final character is played by "tongue lasher," an action figure with the ability to throw out a long, lizardlike tongue. The punch line is that all the suspects have conspired in the murder. It's pretty funny.

I'm due at Phrenology, so I have to race off at the end of the day. As I leave, Estelle hands me an envelope. I feel the telltale shape of a "thank you" chocolate frog. Nice. I stuff it in my pocket and rush into work with about a second to spare, just avoiding a blast from Ali. He's keen on punctuality.

I go into the kitchen, dump my backpack, and grab one of the black aprons we all wear, and there's my mother so engrossed in conversation with Anne that she barely registers me. Anne flicks her eyes toward me for half a second: warmth, approval. Big relief. Maybe we'll avoid getting the essential services cut off, after all.

It's an added bonus, my mother being in the café just now; it means there's no chance of Estelle and Janie being spotted when they climb the fence and install Janie in the stables. As I clear tables and juggle crockery, I'm hoping they won't lose the key or forget the alarm code. I'm feeling some qualms about letting them use Oliver's place. Although it wasn't something we discussed, he didn't say I *couldn't* hide someone in there. In an emergency.

It's a busy post-school shift, a blur of Smarties biscuits and milkshakes, so I don't remember Estelle's envelope until hours later when I'm going to bed and I feel it crackle as I get undressed. Inside the envelope with the choco-late frog, now soft from my body heat, is a note. I eat the frog—a bit yuck, because I've just cleaned my teeth—and read the note, which says, in Estelle's backward-sloping writing:

What? My heart is racing. I read it again. I can't believe my eyes. *Love?* She loves me big time? I know these girls are inclined to a bit of hyperbole. And love doesn't exactly mean "love," it's more like "I approve of you big time," or "I'm grateful to you big time," but it's enough to make me worry again about whether I should ask Estelle to the social. I scan my memory, trying to recover the exact words she used that night at her place. "I might be taking someone"…"I'm probably taking someone"…"I think I'm taking someone." Was she just trying to put me off? Or had she actually asked someone? What if she hasn't? Things between us have improved since then, haven't they? And what about disc boy? Maybe he's about to do something useful like move base to the other side of the planet.

When the alarm beeps at five to five it is as though my brain has been sitting awake for some time, just wait-ing for my body to join it. I jump out of bed and pull on track pants and sneakers. There's a scraping noise as the trapdoor cover moves. I put food into Howard's mouth, as planned, and go into the storeroom. Estelle peers down, then puts herself into reverse and climbs on down the ladder. She gives Howard a pat and beams at me, her eyes shining with excitement. Howard, miraculously, doesn't bark.

I've done my homework, too. I know the fourteenth step creaks. I've got a backpack to carry Howard in, and plenty of snacks to shut him up if he's about to bark. I've even oiled the back door, a compulsory Enid Blyton–style maneuver for nighttime escapades.

As we make our way downstairs I nearly fall over when step number thirteen creaks and groans. Aaaagh! I must have counted the landing as "one." I freeze, teeth chattering, slipping Howard a preemptive shut-up snack. Estelle grabs my arm really hard. She's quaking with suppressed nervous giggles. The step creaks again when we step off it. Estelle takes a couple of deep, calming breaths. I make myself count to ten. When I get to six, I hear a door open.

"Dan, is that you?" my mother says.

Estelle grips my arm again. She carefully moves down one step in front of me so she'll be hidden if my mother comes to the upstairs landing.

From who knows where, I manage to dig up a sleepy-sounding voice, despite an adrenaline spike that's nearly blowing my head off.

"Just taking Howard out."

"Do you want me to take him?"

"It's okay, I'm halfway there. Night."

"Night, darling."

Following a splodge of cell phone light, we fly silently through the garden, my heart rate just about returning to normal as we get to Oliver's door, where Janie is waiting for us.

"Did you lock up?" I ask.

I sense some eye-rolling as Janie hands me the key.

"You only reminded me about a hundred times, so, yeah."

Then we're out the gate, up the lane, past Mrs. Da Silva's and into the street around the corner. There's hardly any traffic, and no one around except a few people sleeping on benches as we make our way through the park.

Just before we get to the city a police car cruises toward us. I get Howard out of the backpack and hiss, "We're training." The car slows and pulls up beside us.

"What's he talking about?" Janie starts to bleat, silenced by a nudge from Estelle.

"Everything okay here?" the street-side guy asks.

"Yep. Just out on a training run. For rowing," I say.

"You're a fair way from the river."

"We do an hour's circuit before we get to the boatsheds, then an hour on the water. Five days a week." I shut up, hoping I don't sound as nervous as I feel. Just talking to a policeman makes me feel as guilty as anything.

The two of them look us over carefully. We are obviously not drunk or otherwise trashed.

They ask to see our backpacks. Janie offers hers for inspection. All she's got in it is clothes, which could conceivably be to change into after training, and food. What are they looking for? Spray paint? Automatic weapons? Large quantities of class-A drugs?

They exchange a couple of quiet words and even if they suspect something is amiss, they must decide there are bigger problems than us in the throbbing metropolis.

"Good luck with the rowing," the driving one says before they take off.

It's cost us a few minutes, so now we have to run.

The city is busier than you'd imagine at five in the morning, when the stars are still out. Deliveries are being made, streets being swept, cleaners roll in and out of buildings. Industrial garbage trucks roar and charge about like armored beasts. And there are quite a few clubbers on the ugly end of a great night out.

We get to the depot with about a minute to spare and wave Janie off with kisses from Estelle and "break a leg" from me.

Estelle and I walk back home, coconspirators. We are elated. And starving. It's still cold and dark and we're falling over ourselves laughing as we sift through the morning—Howard knew not to bark, what a champ...Your mother waking up! I thought we were dead for sure...Training?

Where did that come from?...What were they even looking for?...What if they'd asked us anything about rowing?... She'd better win, after getting us up before dawn...

We cut through the park diagonally, then cross Victoria Parade and run to the closest shops on Gertrude Street. There's a café taking a delivery from a patisserie van. Pooling our coins, we talk our way into an early coffee and get an almond croissant to share.

We perch in a tram shelter, knees up, Howard curled between us like a hot water bottle.

"What's your credit on the film?" I ask.

"Writer, executive producer, and special effects."

"That was you? The noise when they cut the head off? It was gruesome."

"Five years of cello lessons," she says modestly.

"What happens if she wins and they want to buy it?"

"We haven't exactly figured that out yet."

"They won't be able to do a contract with her, because of her age."

"It's in the category of brilliantly good problem. We'll worry about it when it happens."

I can't believe my luck, having all this uninterrupted Estelle time. She is utterly beautiful, even more so with her messy hair, slob clothes, and not a scrap of makeup. Her eyes are as clear as the lightening morning sky. As usual, I cannot stop looking at her.

She wipes her mouth self-consciously. "Have I got froth?"

I want to say, *I love you big time*, too, but I settle for, "I'm just admiring your beauty," which she chooses to take as flippancy.

"Very funny." She brushes a finger along my chin. "Crumbs. Come on, we'd better get going."

It's still about half an hour before anyone is ever up at my place, but she's right, it's getting lighter by the second.

I offer her my hand. She takes it.

"I'm ready for more sleep," she says, standing up. "Too early for running."

We walk home in silence, stopping in the alley next to the back gates.

"You know, the social…" I begin.

"Don't start about the DJ again. Just because I'm tired doesn't mean I'll cave."

"Sure—it's just…"

"Did I tell you I found the best dress to wear?"

"No."

Remembering I'm a boy, with all that usually implies about fashion awareness, she looks apologetic. "You're probably not even vaguely interested."

"Of course I am," I lie.

"Okay, so strapless, dark gray silk organza with a fitted bodice and the skirt has black netting underneath. It's gorgeous."

"That's great, I just wanted to…"

She is listening. I clench my jaw to stop my teeth chattering and am momentarily distracted by a baby magpie warbling.

"You just wanted...?"

Howard makes a disgruntled sound. He's as impatient with me as I am.

I dig about in my pack and find a snack to keep Howard quiet. There's a bit of fluff-covered courage in there, too.

"I just wanted to ask if you'd like to come with me."

She looks at me.

"To the social."

"Oh, Dan," she says, sounding... is it disappointed, or just embarrassed? "I've already asked someone. I'm sorry."

"That's cool. No big deal."

"But thanks. Heaps."

"Sure. No problem."

When we go into the kitchen there's already something cooking. I hear water running in the downstairs bathroom. Why is my mother up so early?

I hurry Estelle out of the kitchen just as the bathroom door at the end of the hallway starts to open, and manage to bustle her into the front sitting room and start untying my shoes with apparent nonchalance as my mother emerges.

"Dan! Where have you been?"

"Running."

"You left before six?" The tone is high-pitched incredulity.

"Er, yeah."

"But you run in the afternoons."

"Usually, but not always."

"And what's Howard doing in a backpack?"

Oops.

"He's got a bit of a sore leg."

"So why didn't you leave him at home?"

"I thought he'd enjoy the—scenery."

"In the dark? How long have you been gone? Your bed was stone cold."

"Not that long. How come you're up so early anyway?"

"I'm making stuff for Phrenology."

She fixes me with her X-ray *I haven't got to the bottom of this* look, which doesn't augur well, and goes back to the kitchen.

I grab Estelle from the sitting room, where she's frozen, eyebrows up in alarm position, and we race back upstairs. Before she climbs the ladder she gives me a quick hug.

"We couldn't have done it without you."

23

The final piece of the great Sydney con is the phone call from Janie's "mother" telling school she won't be in today. We appeal to Lou—levelheaded, deep-voiced Lou—who pulls an Academy Award–worthy performance out of nowhere. So, done and dusted, and all we need to do now is wait to hear if Janie wins.

As the day wears on, Estelle has checked her phone three gazillion times. She has to keep checking, because it's on silent. So when the text finally comes through during the last period Estelle is so wired for it that she screams, pretends she's seen a wasp, and is told to act her age. And after all that the message is: **nearly there, have fun in math ha ha x**☺

After school Estelle waits for me as though it's a regular thing that we walk home together. She nibbles at her sleeve and invites me to put in an earbud and listen to some Hot Chip. Our shoulders and upper arms bump together from time to time and it feels, to me at least, like we are joined by the sort of electric charge you see in old horror movies when they're doing a brain transplant. She seems oblivious or immune to any such effects. But maybe I do from the outside, too.

"Do you want to come to mine and see how she goes?" Estelle asks.

Do I?

"I'll get us a DVD," I say, trying to remind my heart that it's a super-fit muscle and not a drum getting the crap beaten out of it.

"Cool."

I go inside, do a cursory sniff of armpits. Okay. I lick the back of my hand, let the spit dry, and smell it—apparently a better breath checker than breathing into your cupped hand. Also okay. I let Howard come with me to Oliver's to choose a DVD.

"What do you think about *Donnie Darko*? It's one of her favorites. And if you like that movie, you can always enjoy a new viewing. And it'll be one more thing we have in common."

Howard barks his approval/disapproval.

"If, by that, you mean I shouldn't know she likes the film, you're right. If you mean we're going to bond over the film, also right. If you're wondering how I reconcile the two positions, I don't know."

He does the worried whiny noise. It either means he wants to pee or he thinks I'm morally compromised.

The credits are rolling on the film, we've finished a pizza, and I'm wondering if I can ask Estelle who she's taking to the social. I'm assuming it's disc boy. I can't decide if I can bear hearing about it or not. Now we're in a new phase of our relationship—i.e., we *have* a relationship—she might think she can confide in me and tell me how much she likes him. I definitely can't handle that. Probably better not to know. I've just decided it's definitely better not to know when a text beeps into Estelle's phone: **didn't win, crazy, love ya x**

Estelle rings straight back and we get the lowdown. Even though Janie didn't win, the audience loved her film—lots of laughs and big applause. One of the reasons it couldn't win was the copyright problems caused by the cast: Barbie, Ken, and the Power Rangers.

"I didn't even think of that," says Estelle.

"Neither," yells Janie, "but the honcho guy loves my vision. He said stay in touch."

"We love your vision, too," says Estelle.

"Who's we?" Janie wants to know.

"Me and Dan," Estelle says, smiling at me.

"Don't miss the bus," I yell.

We're still buzzing when we hear the sound of a key in the front door. Estelle jumps up in alarm.

"Someone's breaking in. And they've got a key!"

I look around for a weapon and pick up the remote—not as deadly as I might have wished, but it was that or a large book on someone called Cy Twombly.

We both stand, ready for action.

But it's only Vivien. She comes in with her arms full of folders and a laptop bag slung across her chest.

"Mum!?" says Estelle, trying to recover from the shock.

"I do live here, darling."

"But it's Friday. You're never home till late."

"Well, *sorry*, but the gallery's bedlam. I can't escape my phone and I need some clear space to *think*."

She turns around. Someone is coming up behind her as she takes her key from the door.

Estelle's face turns white as she hears, "Vivien, hi."

Panic in her eyes, Estelle silently mouths "crap" and hisses, "It's Janie's mum! What do we do?"

I shrug, helpless. For someone who has foreseen this very problem there isn't a single lightbulb flickering on.

"Sarah. Come in," says Vivien.

"What are you doing here at this hour?" asks Sarah.

"Escaping from work, so I can get some work done."

"Good luck. I won't come in, but can you give this to Janie? One night without a toothbrush is fine, but two? That's going to get furry."

"I didn't even know she was coming. I'm *so* sorry—negligent mother! My headspace is entirely taken up with the show. Estelle, where's Janie? Sarah's brought her toothbrush."

I can see Estelle is as much at a loss as I am. Is she wondering whether she can try, "in the shower"..."in the garden"... "gone through the back of the wardrobe"...?

"And she's staying tomorrow, too? That's great company for Stell while I'm so busy," says Vivien.

Janie's mother is now standing in the hallway, looking confused.

"But...she was here last night."

"No...Thursday? No! She wasn't, was she, Estelle?" Vivien is momentarily concerned that she has vagued out so completely on household arrangements that she doesn't even know who is staying here.

"Sarah, do come in for a bit. I haven't seen you for ages. You can tell me what I should know about school. Our children. Life. The universe..."

Estelle knows she can't fake it. Vivien would eventually recall last night's dinner, and that Janie wasn't there.

Right now would be a perfect time for me to step in and save the day, but I still don't have a clue what to say.

Janie's mother is reading Estelle's concerned look.

"My god, what is it?"

Estelle and I look at each other, recognizing a dead-end street when we see it.

"Where is she?"

"She's fine," says Estelle. "There's absolutely no need to worry."

"What on earth do you mean, Estelle? Where's Janie?" asks Vivien, ushering Sarah in and closing the door.

"She's about to catch a bus home, very, very soon."

"Very," I add. Truly dismal, but it's all I've got.

"What bus? From where?" asks Vivien, snapping with impatience.

"Actually—Sydney," says Estelle. "Please don't get mad."

Janie's mum sits down as though her leg bones have gone wobbly.

Five minutes later my mother is sitting in front of us, too, and the interrogation is on in earnest.

It's fair to say they are angry, furious even, and without having to confer, Estelle and I realize it's best to just roll over on this one. There are times when mounting a defense only makes things worse. So we agree we've been stupid, irresponsible, immature, deceitful, and encouraged a friend in risk-taking behavior.

Once Sarah has spoken to Janie on the phone and reassured herself that she is indeed okay, Estelle attempts to exonerate me from the crime.

"It was all planned before we even told Dan. All he tried to do was make sure we were safe walking to the bus depot. He even tried to talk us out of it."

"We don't need any convincing that you and Janie are

the evil masterminds here," says Vivien from narrowed purple lips.

"And I don't care how small a role you played in this, Dan, it's not okay," my mother says. "And when I asked you a direct question about it this morning, you lied."

"It wasn't exactly lying," I begin. My words freeze as I register how angry she is. We head for home.

"You're grounded for a month and it's not negotiable," Vivien is telling Estelle

"But what about the social?"

The last thing I hear is Vivien saying, "You must be joking!"

By the time we get home my mother's anger has turned to disappointment, which is a lot harder to handle.

We sit at the kitchen table and she's looking at me, her eyes filling with tears. I feel so low. I'm situated somewhere between the sole of my shoe and a grimy sidewalk, between a snake's intestines and the sliding desert sand, or even lower, between sewer lines and the earth's burning core. I was also between a rock and a hard place, in a tight spot, in over my head, in deep...

"Are you even listening to me?"

Uh-oh, yelling *and* sad. I tune back in and pay full attention.

The agreeing with accusations continues. I feel just like Howard when he rolls over, stomach up, legs in the air. I am your abject subject. You are so, so right—I am so, so wrong. And the thing is, I agree with her. She feeds me the exact arguments I had given Estelle and Janie about why it wasn't safe for a young, unaccompanied girl to go to Sydney; why it wasn't okay to lie about your age; why there needs to be a relationship of trust between parents and children. On this last point, our paths split. Parents don't need to know absolutely everything, but if they're likely to find out anyway you might as well come clean up front.

Listening and nodding, I realize that I, myself, could be a perfectly plausible parent. I know all the lines.

"I'm not going to ground you, Dan." My mother is *finally* winding up. "God knows we need you to keep your job." This prompts a fresh round of tears. I don't point out that grounding usually only applies to fun social activities. She's having a wallow, and who am I to stop her?

"I know you're a sensible boy and I'm glad you tried to talk the girls out of this stupidity. I'm going to look on this as an aberration. I need to trust you. It's the only way we can get on together."

I nod, encouraged, maintaining my best solemn and guilty expression. It's looking good; I'm getting off pretty lightly.

"And you are extremely lucky this didn't cause any damage to Oliver's place."

Here, I really have to bite my tongue, but I nod again, wondering what on earth damage one girl sleeping on his sofa for a couple of hours could possibly have caused.

"Anything could have happened. She could have started a fire. She could have left the place open and vulnerable to burglary."

As I imagine Janie spontaneously combusting and setting the whole place alight, my mother trails off. I don't think she's convinced even herself that Janie could have done much harm.

"You are going to write a letter of apology to Janie's parents for your part in this plan."

"Do you really think that's a good idea? Won't it just prolong the pain?"

She quenches my objection with a look containing about a cubic kilometer of icy water.

So I write:

Dear Ms. Preston and Mr. Bacon,

I am writing to apologize for my part in facilitating Janie's trip to Sydney to attend the awards ceremony for the "Hanging on the Telephone" competition.

I truly regret helping her in this potentially dangerous undertaking. Anything could have happened but thank god it didn't.

Please accept my apologies and the assurance that I will speak up more forcefully against it

if a similar scheme is ever planned with my
knowledge. Which I am sure it will not be.

Yours faithfully,

Dan Cereill

I feel like a proper dick, but I can live with that. Embarrassment is one of my primary dispositions.

It occurs to me that the letter is a bit premature; there could still be a fatal bus crash on the highway. I'll hold off posting it till the morning. I also realize that, miraculously, the part the attic played in the great escape has gone undetected.

My stomach steps in and helps change the subject by producing a roar of hunger. We cook pasta and have it with some leftover Napoli sauce. As we season the food with a little subdued, polite conversation, I notice the kitchen is full of new biscuits and slices and things.

"This looks good."

"Ali said he's happy to try a few different things while I'm doing the cooking."

"I'm glad you got the job."

"I wouldn't exactly call it a job."

"Eight weeks."

"It's better than nothing."

"And it might lead to something."

"Yeah, eight weeks of pay." She sounds bitter. Who can

blame her? It's easy to forget how different her life used to be only a few months ago.

"I really admire the way you're coping with all this," I say, feeling awkward. Someone has to give her a bit of encouragement. And there's only me here.

She hugs me. I take Howard out for his bedtime pee and head up for an early night.

Shutting my door, I hear a loud whisper coming from the storeroom hatch. "Dan, are you there?"

Estelle is peering down from a crack in the trapdoor cover, which she now opens wider.

"Can I come down?"

"Sure."

I check my door is locked and put on some music to muffle our talking.

When Estelle climbs down, I can see she's been crying.

"Do you think Janie's okay? My mother's made me so worried she'll get assaulted on the bus, or there'll be a crash, or something else horrible. And it'll be my fault for not stopping her."

"It was her decision. She would've gone anyway."

"She couldn't have afforded to without the money I gave her."

"Well, maybe you stopped her from hitchhiking."

"Maybe," she says, allowing herself to be half comforted.

"She's going to be fine. The only dangerous thing on Janie's horizon is her parents."

"My mother's taking back my dress!" Estelle says between hiccups and a fresh welling of tears. "She's so horrible."

I have no idea what she's talking about.

"The gray dress. The one I told you about. That I love, and there'll never be another one like it!"

"That's—bad."

"Oooh, what are these?" Estelle has wandered over to my desk and is looking into the box of little carvings Adelaide had left my mother.

"Insects. Frogs. Little weird dudes."

"They're cute," she sniffs.

"Take one. Any one you like."

She smiles at me.

"Just to borrow. It'll cheer me up."

She looks through the collection and chooses a little fat guy sitting on a frog. It's my favorite, too, but she's welcome to it. It's another sign of how compatible we are. If only she realized.

"I just hate how we're supposed to be so independent and show initiative, but only on their terms. The minute you really show some initiative they just want to squash you back into the kid-shaped box."

"Are you still grounded for a month?"

"In theory, yeah. But I can visit you. And there's always the tree."

"Not the tree, please."

"You've got to stop worrying so much," she says. "How much trouble did you end up getting into?"

"It wasn't too bad, I guess because things here are borderline catastrophe anyway, so other stuff sort of shrinks."

"Any yelling?"

"Some."

"My mother screamed her lungs out when you guys left. I'm not kidding—she just about lost her voice. She pretends to be so rational in front of other people, but she's the full nut job when it's just us. And of course it's all about her. I *ruined* her whole night! She was so *stressed* just when she needed calm *thinking* time! What a drama queen."

Estelle heads for the ladder.

"I'd rather stay with you and Howard, but I'm probably up for at least one more serve of how *irresponsible* and *inconvenient* I am."

In a volley of texts I find out when Janie arrives back—on time and unscathed—to be promptly grounded by her furious parents. While she and Estelle are lying low, I have a challenging social engagement that needs my full attention. I'm introducing Fred and Lou.

We arrange to meet up at Richmond Gardens shopping complex and see a movie, so if they don't like each other at least no one's wasted too much time.

Fred is already in the foyer when I arrive. Lou arrives a minute after me. I suspect she's been in a surveillance position at Skittle City Bowling on the mezzanine level, waiting for me to appear. When I introduce them, they size each other up. Lou cuts to the chase.

"Our social is in two weeks and Dan thinks I should ask you. I trust his opinion and he says I wouldn't hate spending some time with you—so would you like to come?"

Fred can't believe his ears.

"That's very direct," he says.

Lou gives a Lou shrug.

"We both know why we're here. I don't do coy. If we sort this out, we can forget about it and enjoy the film."

"Okay. Yes. Of course I'll come," says Fred. "What date is it?"

"Two and a bit weeks. The twenty-fourth."

"That's even better. My stepmother is trying to line me up with some friend's daughter that night. I've resisted so far, but this gives me a solid out."

"My mother's been on my back about asking a friend's son. So this lets me off the hook, too. I can hardly take two people to the social."

Fred says, "Your mother's name—it's not Maggie, is it?"

"Are you kidding? You mean your stepmother is Harriet? From the history department?"

"Yep."

"Mercy me, you're the charming boy," Lou says, smiling.

"And you are the delightful girl."

The realization prompts an intense discussion of probability theory. Not classic first date chitchat, but it breaks the ice. I remember they both love Philip Pullman's books, so when I throw that into the arena there's no stopping them.

When Fred goes to pick up some film flyers, Lou takes the opportunity for a quick aside. "You're right. He's nice. Kind of like a short, nervy version of you. And his pimples aren't even that bad."

It's looking like love must be shortsighted, at the very least.

Fred comes back to ask who wants a choc-top. Lou says she'll have one if they've got boysenberry. Snap. It's Fred's favorite, too. Now the compatibility-o-meter is rating off the charts.

The minute Lou is out of earshot, putting her wrapper in a bin, Fred gives me his feedback.

"She's got a lot of style. And she doesn't do the strange sort of girl talk where you don't know what they mean. And the pimples aren't even that bad."

Snap again.

I should have predicted what happens next. As we sit down I make sure they're next to each other. The minute the last choc-top bite is swallowed they're holding hands. Five minutes into the feature I hear the gentle, slurpy noise of kissing.

If you've ever sat next to two friends making out in the dark, you'll know it's a bit uncomfortable.

"Guys," I say, "I can't see that well. I'm going to sit a bit closer to the screen."

No response.

When I see them after the movie they've already made plans to catch up next weekend.

I'm wasted doing waitstaff work—I should obviously be setting up a dating agency.

24

All Lou wants to talk about is Fred—she can't get over meeting a boy she likes who likes her, too. All Estelle and Janie want to talk about is the social—they can't get over the injustice of not being allowed to go.

We sit together now since Lou helped out by being Janie's "mother." I've been a friend catalyst. That's a first.

"Punished for daring to be creative," says Janie. "That's probably against some UN convention or something."

"I think the problem was more *where* you were being creative," says Uyen.

"I'm sick of living with people who are so hung up on details," says Estelle.

"Maybe we should go to the social anyway," says Janie.

"Come! You can meet Fred," says Lou.

"That would be great. If we could get away with it," says Estelle. "But we can't."

Janie's got the mad look in her eyes. "Why don't we just do it?"

"Because they'd kill us," says Estelle.

"And would that be any worse than missing out on the only social we've ever had?"

"Could you get out without them knowing?" asks Lou.

"Estelle could," says Janie, fixing me with can't-escape-it laser eyes.

"Not down the tree," I say.

"Dan, you've got to get over this irrational fear of the tree," says Estelle, sounding very much like her mother.

Janie's look of growing concentration and calculation is starting to worry me.

"You know they always start out really strict and really cross when you've done something wrong...?" she says.

"Yeah, then you get the thin edge of the wedge."

"Exactly. So, what about, 'I know I'm grounded, but seeing as I'm missing the whole entire social, how about you let me have a little sleepover with Estelle?'"

They look at me expectantly.

"You both want to go down the tree?"

"Have you got a better plan?" asks Estelle.

"Stay home?"

"Dan!"

"What do we wear, though?" says Janie. "Seeing as how the mean mothers have taken our dresses back."

Estelle smiles. "Dan's attic is full of boxes, and the boxes are full of all these fantastic old things. Including clothes."

"So, vintage? Okay, I like it," says Janie.

"Even if they find out and ground you for two months afterward, at least you will have been to the social," says Lou.

"If I did that my parents would ground me for a year," says Uyen.

"We'll get life, minimum, if they catch us," says Estelle.

"So, we don't get caught," says Janie with a shrug. "Simple solutions are always the best."

Pittney is glaring at us and warming up to a tantrum if we keep talking, but I can see he's getting himself into big trouble with the quadratic equation he's writing up on the board. I'm ready to distract him with that if he starts being difficult.

"Dan, you can wear one of the cool old suits," says Estelle.

"I'm not going," I say.

"How come?" asks Janie.

"I'm just not."

"You can't not go," says Estelle. "You're on the committee."

"I didn't ask for that job."

"You engineered me and Fred going together. As if I'm going to let you get away with a no-show," says Lou.

It seems about a minute ago I was new here. But now I'm sitting in class with people who actually care whether or not I turn up somewhere. So somehow, in between all the other stuff, things must be going okay. The warm fuzzies quickly evaporate when Pittney starts his dummy spit.

"Mr. Cereill," he booms. "As you already have the attention of half the class, perhaps you would like to continue with the problem at hand?"

Crafty. Obviously hoping to administer a bit of public humiliation. But he's the one messing up, and I know where he's gone wrong. So I walk up to the whiteboard, take the marker, and work through the problem—first going back a few steps to fix up his mistake.

He's not happy.

A couple of kids stick out hands for a lazy high five as I make my way back to my desk. Everyone appreciates a teacher being brought unstuck from time to time. I plead guilty to enjoying the attention, and that's how I miss seeing Jayzo stick his foot out. I go sprawling, bashing my elbow hard on the way down. It's pride coming before a fall in a big way. I create a once-in-a-lifetime spark of camaraderie between Pittney and Jayzo, and I'm reminded that I can never afford to let my guard down with Jayzo.

Estelle and Janie are waiting for me at the gate on the way to our science excursion. We're going to the Royal Botanic Gardens. Drawing dry climate specimens. A thrill a minute.

They're not taking no for an answer about the social escape plan.

While we sit on the tram getting tipped from side to side as it swings along the tracks, Estelle pursues her argument with passion. I look into her serious eyes and have to put all my energy into not showing that I'm completely hers, and I'll basically do whatever on earth she asks of me—legal, illegal, pleasant, painful, moral, immoral, safe, risky, fun, unfun...

She shakes my arm. "Dan, are you even listening? Do you even care?"

Care? Do I even care? I'm right up there with "love you big time," which brings me back to that same old itch: who is disc boy? How serious is the relationship? Is he the reason she's so desperate to get to the social? If I go to the social, how will I be able to stand the sight of them together?

"Dan!"

"Of course I care. I'm just not sure it's such a wise idea."

"We're not about being wise," screams Janie, sharing with the entire tram. "We're not frickin' owls."

"They just want to have some fun," says the old lady sitting opposite, buttoned up in a woolly overcoat and matching beret.

Janie is delighted with the public support. She agrees and starts singing at high volume and low melody the old song about girls just wanting to have fun. Estelle joins in more tunefully, laughing, and the old lady taps her umbrella along. Most fun she's had in a while.

"He's coming around," Estelle says, watching me. "That was a smile."

She links her arm through mine. "Just say yes."

"I'll say yes, so long as you both know what you're risking."

"We do," they say.

Uyen is not convinced. "It's exactly the same con that got you into all this trouble in the first place," she says.

"Not really," says Janie.

I'm with Uyen. "It's a fake sleepover," I say.

"Not *quite*. This time it's a real sleepover. We just won't be there for some of it," says Estelle.

"Won't your parents check up on you?" says Uyen.

"My mother will be at the opening and Dad spends every night on the phone talking business to people in different time zones. He won't come near us."

There's no way I'm going to dissuade them. I think about the letter I've only just written Janie's parents and try to square my conscience with the thought that at least I've made an effort to talk them out of it.

I want to be good, but good is a slippery customer. I decide to settle for being loyal to my friends. Does this make me a pathetic pushover? Good or bad? Right or wrong? Who knows?

We're supposed to find the arid garden, the eucalyptus lawn, or the Californian garden, but mostly people huddle together in the tropical greenhouse for warmth, and light up. Lou and Uyen head for the arid garden. Estelle and I set out in that direction as well, but she's shivering, so the two of us duck into the cactus greenhouse for a defrost booster on the way.

It's so warm in here that the condensation dribbles down the glass surfaces, but all those spikes make the warmth feel dangerous.

"That's better," says Estelle, her teeth still jittery.

I want to put my arms around her and warm her up, but—of course—don't.

"These don't even look like plants," she says, mildly horrified. "They're an affront to the whole plant kingdom."

"They look more like diseases," I agree.

"Tumors."

"Or mutants that formed after the meltdown..."

"Yeah, when plants and slimy things bred..."

"...with barbed wire."

"And they're all nasty," she says, wandering around. "Except you." She's talking to an aloe. "Hello, aloe." She breaks a tip off. "Got any scratches?"

I wish. It would be the high point of my life being dabbed with aloe by Estelle. I'd write a song about it. Or an epic poem. Or a tragedy. Depending on how things turned out.

"Dan?"

I'm somehow leaning against a large spiky beast that's hooked into my jumper.

"Ouch."

"It's trying to eat you. Even though you're quite obviously *not* an insect," says Estelle, attempting to unhook me.

"Oops," she says. "I got the little one unstuck, but it's

pushed you into the big one. Yuck, they're not even leaves, they're like big fat paddles or something."

"It's poking into my back," I say. It's quite painful. I'll be in need of aloe any minute.

"Hold still," she says.

Estelle is in extremely close range now, so holding still is pretty well impossible. Her proximity flicks the switch that reallocates the distribution of blood in my body. Throat constricted, head spinning. Paralyzed. Like dream running, when you can't.

"It's going to be easier if we get your jumper off," she says, and gently starts lifting it up. I raise my arms. It's uncomfortable feeling sexually charged and impaled on cactus spikes at the same time. No doubt it's a popular niche activity in some circles, but not mine.

Reminding myself to keep breathing, I remove my arms slowly from my jumper, duck my head out, and step carefully away from the cactus. I'm stepping into Estelle's arms, which are raised, holding my empty jumper. And I'm about to kiss her—totally without warning, and amazingly I can tell she's expecting it, accepting it—when the foggy glass doors slide open and Uyen and Lou burst in with a rush of cold air.

"*Here* you are."

"We thought you got lost." Is that a knowing look from Lou?

Estelle steps away from me abruptly, letting the jumper drop, still suspended on the cactus.

"I got spiked," I explain.

Estelle lifts my jumper off the cactus. "We're all going to have to get some out. Look."

We stare at the jumper. It's covered in cactus spines.

"It's not so bad," says Lou. "These big spikes are much easier to get out than the little furry ones."

I look at Estelle, but whatever was about to happen escaped through the opened doors.

When I get to Phrenology after school I hardly recognize Ali. He's in the kitchen leaning on a bench, talking to my mother. Smiling. It makes his whole face look different. She's smiling, too. They're talking food and both actually looking...relaxed? What's wrong with this picture? Ali chucks me an apron and tells me to start clearing tables.

Moving from table to table, I notice the little kids are eating my mother's strange face biscuits—grumpy frowns, tongues poking out sideways, twirling moustaches, winks. They're a hit.

We walk home together after my shift and there's more good news. Mrs. Da Silva's niece is getting married and she's ordered a cake: the Marilyn. (Don't ask. It sits on a bed of pink ostrich feathers.) Mrs. Da Silva stayed with them the whole time and didn't let my mother start with the "counseling" caper. They stuck strictly with cake talk, price, and delivery arrangements.

25

Running is usually a good way to forget about everything. Slicing through the world, in the pump, the pounding, the thud, in the blur of images—I shed my worries like itching lizard skins and leave them way behind. The more power and endurance and speed I find, the better I like running. I don't even mind the pain. The stretch and ache past comfort make me feel stronger. There's no thinking, just the machine. Usually. But not today. Today I have the near-miss kiss to contend with.

I know, because I listen, that this is the sort of "issue" girls dissect for hours on end. During class in notes, at lunchtime in urgent huddles, after school on the phone no doubt. What did the smallest look or comment mean? The exhaustive *on the one hand but then again on the other hand* 360-degree no-stone-unturned analysis.

I've run all the way from Fitzroy to the Tan Track that loops around the botanic gardens—back to the scene of the crime. It's already dark and the rush-hour traffic hurtling from the city fugs the air. The Yarra River, mud brown by day, is black, glittering with electric light pouring down from city buildings. I race, crunching along the compressed sandy track, badly in need of a fellow-dissector, a speculator, an interpreter. Fred won't do, his approach would be "ask her." Lou would say the same. The question is, (a) were you really going to kiss me? And (b) if so, what does that mean for me, for you, for the guy you're taking to the social?

Her face as I was about to kiss her was almost too beautiful to bear. I'm surprised my retinas aren't fried. Her expression was open, her message simple and complete: Here I am, I show myself to you. The faraway land was close enough to touch, for half a second.

Or maybe I'm deluded, and it was a humidity-induced mirage, ninety percent longing, ten percent condensation. And how will I know when I see her again?

It makes me feel tired about how guarded we are the whole time. Without even trying we're ready to make a joke of everything, serving up the day with big dollops of irony and derision and cynicism. As if. Sucked in. Kidding.

When I get home, panting, flicking my sweat-drenched hair out of my eyes, wiping my face into the shoulder of my T-shirt, Howard, my other pressing problem, is waiting for me right inside the front door. He stands stiffly and wags his tail. I scoop him up and carry him down to the kitchen. He doesn't weigh much. "I'm sorry you can't come running anymore," I tell him.

Maybe I can ask my mother for some of the wedding cake money for the vet.

There's something weird happening. An absence of Radiohead. Instead, my mother is playing some old blues music.

"Do you like it?" she asks. "Ali lent it to me."

"A change is as good as a holiday."

I feel around for a diplomatic way to ask about money but come up with nothing.

"Is Dad sending us any money?"

She sits down and starts laughing. It begins as a world-weary chuckle but ends as a genuinely amused belly laugh. I take it as a no. She eventually calms down, taking some deep breaths.

"Do you need something in particular? Is it for the social? I can only suggest the thrift store, sweetie."

"Nah. Just curious."

"I'm sure he'll send something when he can. But he's not working at the moment."

I realize I haven't had to avoid any phone calls for a while. "Where is he?"

"At a 'wellness' retreat in Byron Bay. Getting centered, or earthed, or grounded, or something."

"How long for?"

"A month, he said."

She starts laughing again. "Back to basics. Carry water, chop wood, meditate. Can you imagine?"

"How's he paying?"

"That's the best part. He's organized a deal—they accommodate him, he does a business plan for them."

I wonder if they know he sent his own business bankrupt. Try as I might, I cannot picture my adrenaline-fueled dad leading this kind of life. I can imagine him bustling into some quiet courtyard in his Italian suit and silk tie, cracking jokes. But meditating?

"He'll do a good job," she says.

She's wiping laugh tears with the back of her hand.

"I miss him, Dan. This is exactly the sort of thing he'd do. He'll end up franchising them."

She fixes me with a serious look. I've walked right into a talk trap, totally unaware.

"I'm still cranky about the business, but I knew about..."

Oh no, she's going to talk about sex.

"He was my best friend and...I mean, I guess I knew... stuff."

"Mum. Please." Read the room and shut up.

"Things don't always turn out the way you think they will."

She gives me the attempted mind-read look, but my thought deflector screens are pretty much permanently in place these days.

Can't she dredge the murky depths of her own adolescence and remember how disturbing it is to think of your parents being sexual at all? Regardless of sexuality. And that's a bit of a lightbulb. Parents + sex (straight... gay... any sex) = no-go zone.

I put together a quick self-help "nine stages of how I relate to my father's sexuality" list:

He's straight, but I really don't want to know about it.
The big gay revelation.
Shock.
Disbelief.
Anger.
Embarrassment.
Ambivalence.
Acceptance.
He's gay, but I really don't want to know about it.

In summary, I never wanted to know before, so why should I care now?

Maybe I can write a magazine story about this and get a big cash injection for Howard's operation.

My mother is chopping up a hunk of chocolate. She

makes her own chocolate chips. She says it's more "rustic" than the little buttons you buy in a pack.

"Perhaps I should have talked to you about this, but I've asked him to come and stay with us for a week after his retreat thingy."

What?

"I'm not going to let you two drift apart. And he certainly doesn't want that, either."

"He's the one who pissed off."

"He'll have to explain why things happened the way they did. Which is another good reason for him to spend some time here."

Suddenly not so sure I'm evolving a mature understanding of my father's situation, I feel anxious. I'm not ready to see him. That would mean speaking to him. The end of that conversation is me saying it's okay that he's gone. I just can't put my head in that space. I'm ricocheting like a pinball, from ambivalence back to disbelief and anger, and bouncing around embarrassment again. Just when I thought I was getting somewhere. So much for my insights.

Howard gives a whinging whine that turns into a sharp bark. He's got surgery on his mind.

"I think Howard wants his dinner," my mother says.

And food.

I pat Howard apologetically and try to bend the discussion back to money.

"So, good news about the cake order."

"Just in time to rescue us from the snapping jaws of the bank."

"No cash to splash?"

"None. It'll cover the bills. Almost. And if I can keep doing some work for Phrenology when Anne gets back, we might just be able to keep our heads above water."

"That's great."

"You know what? It really is." She looks genuinely pleased.

Pittney corners us two days later about the social to tell us we're getting to the "business end" of the planning and demands to know what exactly we have "finalized."

All we really have finalized is a risky "getting there" plan for Estelle and Janie, and that's only if they manage the sleepover con, which looks to me like an outside chance. Apart from that, not much is solid except the venue— the gym.

By the end of lunchtime I cave and we book the year-twelve band Vile Bodies. The transposable parentheses are being difficult about refreshments, so we ask if they'd like to take over that area and they say (omigod) (only) (like) (so) (totally). So now everyone's happy.

No Radiohead again when I get home. Salsa. My mother's grooving around the kitchen while she cooks. I personally don't like seeing parents dance; it's unnatural. But I can see it's a good sign. I'm sure it has something to do with her getting out and about in the world with other human beings. Like Oliver said, good for her brain-health.

"I've said I'll go with Ali to his twenty-year class reunion."

Twenty years out of school. That is so old.

"That's nice of you." Go figure.

"But, Dan, because of the lead time for Mrs. Da Silva's niece's wedding cake..."

"Yes..." I sense a favor about to be asked.

"All the layers, and marinating the fruit...it means the last layer will have to be cooked that night."

"No problem. I'll keep an eye on it."

"You'll have to be utterly reliable, to the minute, or everything's ruined."

I try not to roll my eyes. Of course I understand this. Have I not lived through the product development, the cake trials, the advanced testing, the refining, the perfecting, the getting rid of clients?

"Dan! Don't drift."

"I'm listening! I can turn the oven off. I'll remember. When is it?"

"That's the thing. It's the night of your dance."

"Oh. That's okay."

"But I've worked out the timing. I can put it in to be cooked by midnight. So long as you're home by midnight it'll be fine."

"Consider it done."

"It's possible I'll be home by then but it depends what sort of night it turns out to be."

"I understand." But I don't really. She's doing Ali the big favor, surely she should be able to cut and run when it suits her? She hugs me. Howard wags his tail, thumping it hard on the mat. Normally he jumps around barking if there's any hugging going on. My mother notices.

"Are you tired, little doggy?"

I wish I could tell her exactly what Howard's problem is, but the last thing she needs is something new to worry about just when it seems the clouds are parting.

I give Howard an ear rub while my mother puts food on the table. We're having one of my favorite dinners— piles of roast vegetables with homemade pesto. And there's apple crumble for dessert.

When I carry Howard outside for a bedtime pee, Oliver is arriving home and he's not alone.

"Hey, man, this is Em. Em, Dan."

"Hi."

Em looks scarily cool. She comes over and grabs a handful of my hair.

"Aha! Yes, I think we can do something with that."

I get a warm bro glow, realizing Oliver must have spoken about me to Em.

"House still standing? No burgs?"

"Everything's fine. I let a friend sit in there for a few hours on her way to Sydney."

"That's cool. Okay, see you when we surface."

"Night."

≫≪

While I sit on the back steps waiting for Howard to select a suitable place to pee—it's quite a ritual—I hear a door opening next door and Vivien saying an extremely firm "no."

"But I wouldn't be leaving the house at all," says Estelle.

"Save your breath. Jamie may certainly not come over here. Grounding precludes all social activities, here or elsewhere."

If anger and volume are anything to go by, they're well into the argument.

"We're already missing our social," says Estelle.

"There'll be other school dances."

"Not if I die. Then I will never have been to a proper school dance. In my entire life."

"Don't be dramatic."

"So I'll be all alone, with no one to comfort me on the tragic loss of my one and only social. And you're happy with that!"

"Perfectly. Your father will be here. You'll be fine."

"Fine!"

A door slams. Vivien exhales loudly; it sounds as though she's smoking.

"How sharper than a serpent's tooth it is to have a thankless child, or whatever," she says to the night.

I'm not surprised to hear the trapdoor cover grating open a little while later.

"Knock, knock, are you busy?"

I go into the storeroom. "Nah, come on down."

I expect Estelle to be upset, but she obviously knows her mother better than I do. She expects to lose a few battles, it's all part of a strategic wearing-down campaign. She is confident that her mother, and Janie's, will give up, exhausted, by the night of the social.

"Especially if I can bring home an A or an A-plus on something in the next few days, and I fill the house with Yo-Yo Ma."

"Rap?"

"Cello."

She looks right at home curled up on my bed next to Howard, her hair wet, wearing striped PJs. Ironically, she would be the perfect person to talk to about her.

If I had any guts I'd broach the near-miss kiss, or, better still, initiate a new kiss, but instead I start telling Estelle about my father. The whole story—bankruptcy, gayness, Byron Bay. She listens completely, never taking her serious eyes from my face.

It's definitely gutless, but maybe it's also a reply of sorts: me saying here I am; I show myself to you.

"Interesting," she says. "It's like he's having his teenage years now, instead of back then. Because he and your mother got together so early, before he knew who he'd turn out to be."

"Yeah, I guess."

"He must have really loved her to want to get married and have you, even though somewhere inside he must also have known it mightn't be right for him."

"Why do you think it took him so long?"

She shakes her head.

"Imagine how hard it would be. Years ago you land on married-daddy planet. Then you have to turn around to the whole world and say, actually, guys, I took a wrong turn—didn't mean to come here—I'm supposed to be way over there."

"He should have known sooner."

"Maybe he did, but by that time you were a family. It sounds like you were a happy family."

"We were."

It's a relief to remember that's still true.

"Years could go by. He probably couldn't bear to hurt you. Then, in the middle of the big meltdown, maybe he thought, jump, it's now or never."

She's good. Are all girls natural psychologists? Everything she says lightens my load of worry bricks.

When I tell her about the unopened birthday present she even has a theory about that. I didn't open it at first because I was angry. It was a simple withholding, a rejection of him. But the longer I leave it unopened, the more it symbolizes. So wrapped up in there, with whatever, is the hope that magically, improbably, impossibly, my father can give me something that will make everything okay again. And for as long as it's unopened, that hope is alive.

I'm not kidding, she could charge money for this.

26

In freakishly fast time there are only five days until the social, then four, then three—everything seems to be organized—then two days to go...

And two things happen.

The first one is that there's a rush on ticket sales. All the undecideds, too-cools, and can't-afford-its unexpectedly commit. Like an invisible message received by the herd, going to the social is the accepted thing to do.

It may have something to do with Vile Bodies, whose reputation is firming based on decent performances at a couple of recent parties.

Which makes the second thing that happens two days before the social even worse. And it's completely my fault.

I somehow manage to collide, in classic *running around the corner from opposite directions too fast* manner, with the lead guitarist. This seems to annoy him. A lot. He's extremely fond of himself.

When I say sorry he screams abuse at me, so I tell him to chill and he says, "Chill on this, arsehole," and swings a punch in my direction.

Being a dedicated fan of pain avoidance, I manage to duck and swerve on a rush of pure fear, and his punch lands on a metal locker door. I fall off the unexpectedly-popular-entrepreneur pedestal in one loud, agonized expletive.

Jayzo gets the call in English.

"You've really done it now, dickhead," he says to me. "You broke his meta-something."

"Metacarpal?" asks Lou.

"Yeah, that," he replies.

"One of these bones," says Lou, pointing to the back of her hand.

"No guitar for a month," Jayzo says. He's enjoying it. "All gigs are off."

A gasp of horror sweeps around me.

"Are you saying we've got no band? For the social?" asks Janie.

"That's right. All thanks to him," says Jayzo.

"He punched *me*," I remind people in feeble defense. No one cares about the details.

I'm the prize spoiler of all fun, skewered by the dagger stares of the entire class.

I more or less expect hatred from Jayzo, but even my friends are turning on me.

"They were going to play our song," says Lou.

"We don't have a song," I say, deliberately obtuse.

"Mine and Fred's," she says. "Obviously."

"Mine and Fred's, mine and Fred's," I echo childishly.

"What, are you jealous? Can't be happy for us? Set us up and then regret it?"

I can hardly defend myself by saying I'm so self-obsessed I've barely given them a second thought.

"None of the above," I say. "I just didn't think you of all people would go so teenage on me."

She looks at me. Very unimpressed.

"You're lashing out because you're under siege. I get that. But just try to play nice, and remember who your friends are," she says, walking off.

Isn't it a bit early for them to have a song? Already? They'll be married with children by next year if they keep going at this rate.

Estelle and Janie corner me at the lockers.

"Aren't we having a hard enough time about the social without you doing this?" Estelle asks.

"It was an accident."

"Bad timing, Dan, really bad timing," says Janie, digging the tip of her pen into someone's lock.

"You two might not even be able to come!"

They glare at me.

"Thanks, I feel so much better now," Estelle says.

"I can still organize music," I say, wondering how.

"Good luck with that," says Janie. "That gym sucks up sound like the Grand Canyon. The very least you need is a damn kick-arse sound system."

I think about the large plastic radio I have at home. It was Adelaide's. One of the earliest FM models. It struggles to pick up Triple J.

"It's about the atmosphere," says Estelle. "Every girl will be walking in there looking for a night to remember."

She gets a misty-eyed look, dreaming of disc boy, no doubt. I give an exasperated sigh.

"Hey, we're the ones who are annoyed here," Estelle says. "You're the one who's messed things up."

If there were any justice in the universe, this is where I'd step in, stunning everyone with my hitherto modestly-never-mentioned guitar brilliance, and they'd go wild and insist *I* play in the band at the social. And Estelle would fall for me. Maybe she'd join me up onstage...

"Could you not stare into space like we're boring you? A sorry would be nice."

"Of course I'm sorry, but—"

But nothing. It isn't worth it. No more "it wasn't my fault." I just have to wear it.

"You're up against a thousand sleepovers with romcoms about proms. We're looking for the director's cut," says

Janie, in a soothing *let me explain* tone. "All the good bits left in."

"Including the band," says Estelle.

At lunchtime Dannii comes toward me with an angry posse and starts throwing the parentheses around like weapons.

"I totally cannot believe what I hear. Omigod we've got orders. Things that like *so* cannot be canceled," she says.

"That's okay, it's not like the social's been called off," I try.

She rolls her eyes at the posse, and they roll theirs back in response.

"It'll be so totally random with like no music," she says.

"I'll get music."

"You better or you're a full gay loser."

They turn on a collective (chunky black lace-up) heel and walk off.

By the end of the day I've been made to feel bad a hundred ways, but nobody gives me a harder time than Jayzo. Naturally. He's loving it, and making a big deal about the guitarist being his friend.

So after needling me most of the day, he waits till the last class, English, picks up one of the taggers' heavy-duty Sharpies, grabs my hair, and tags my face. He's covered most of it before I manage to get hold of the pen and shove him off. I'm sent out to wash it off, but it's permanent marker and it won't budge.

219

I stand up voluntarily in front of a class for the second time ever. When the jeering, whistling, and abuse simmer down, I reassure them all that I'll fix things. I'll organize something as good as or better than what we've lost. And I'll do it by tomorrow night. I'm not going to let them down. They should trust me. Believe me. The social is on.

I walk home alone, mulling. My problems are like waves—just as one disappears with a snarl and a hiss there's another shaping up to knock me down.

I try booking agents first. In three calls it's pretty clear that even the most pathetic cover bands are way out of our budget league. That leaves jukeboxes. These are affordable, but offer dodgy music selection and sound quality. But beggars can't be choosers. I make some more calls. Despite feeling uncomfortable about settling for second best, it turns out second best isn't even available on one day's notice. It must be party season or something. The only thing I track down that I can afford is a kids' jukebox loaded with Wiggles music. It's not going to cut it with angry fifteen-year-olds. Now it's five thirty, businesses are shutting, I'm talking to answering machines, and I'm dead. I've come up with nothing. Good odds on me being a casualty of crowd violence by around eight thirty tomorrow morning.

Maybe my mother will have a solution, like sending me to a new new school, or getting me into a witness protection program or something.

But she has new problems of her own. So much so that

she barely blinks at the sight of my ink-covered face. She needs a crown. The tooth kind, not the head kind. It's going to cost megabucks. The news has sent her into a misery spin. All her frantic balancing of bills and debt is tipping over.

"You know what I feel like doing? I feel like getting a flint and a hammer and just knocking the stupid thing out like Tom Hanks did in that movie when he was on the island."

"It was an ice-skate blade and a rock," I say.

"Bring it on!"

It's so preposterous it makes us both laugh. But I see she's really worried and probably not up for a *help teenage son sort out consequences of his own idiotic actions* session. I'm relieved when the phone rings and it's Oliver saying I can come over for my haircut.

When I start explaining why my face is tagged, the whole screwup of the century and my useless attempts at solving it come burbling out.

They listen sympathetically as Em hacks into my hair in a seemingly haphazard but very confident way. She chooses bits of hair, picks them up, twists them, cuts them in no apparent order, lets them drop, and chooses again.

"Voilà," she says, putting the scissors down when I think she's about half done. I look into the mirror. My hair is a complete mess, long and short bits all over the place. But

I take my cue from the two satisfied expressions smiling back at me and say thanks.

"Did I tell you she was good?" asks Oliver.

"Yeah. You did."

"Never, never, never brush it," says Em. "Ever." She hands me a tube of hair goo. "Rub a bit of this through to mess it up after you wash it. But don't wash it too often."

I nod as though I understand what the hell she means, and make a mental note to ask Estelle about it.

"And with the dance," she says. "I can maybe do your music."

I nearly fall off the stool. Is my life about to be saved?

"What's the venue?" she asks.

"The school gym. But it's tomorrow night. Are you sure?"

"I'm not booked for anything till next weekend."

I know from Oliver that Em is *the* famous DJ Pony. Posters advertising her gigs are plastered around everywhere.

When I mention the amount of money we have to pay the band, she laughs.

"That's cool, we'll put it toward speakers hire."

"What about your—payment—fee?"

"Well, you know, any friend of Oliver's...I'll do you a freebie, lad."

My face must be a picture of complete disbelief.

"It's not a big deal," she says. "I won't make the music, I'll just plug in one of my playlists. A dancy one. And maybe get some lights. Fluorescent tubes in wire cages don't do it for me."

I look at them, unable to make sense of such good luck. Oliver is like a miracle—a kind of hip older-brother fairy-godmother style-guru hybrid.

"I don't mind the tagged face," Em says as I leave. "It's kinda urban warrior. Cute."

After another scrub there's still no change to the inked face. It might as well be a tattoo.

Back in my room I hear a knocking from above and Estelle climbs down the storeroom ladder. She's brought makeup remover.

"I'm sorry about today," she says. "I wasn't very supportive. Or—supportative?"

"Supportive."

She's putting the lotion on my face. It's dissolving my concentration but having no effect on the ink, apparently. She stands back, puzzled. "This even takes off stage makeup." She stops abruptly, looking at me. "Your hair! It's amazing. How did I not notice? You have sharpened right up since the beginning of term."

"Thanks. I've got replacement music for the social."

"That's great. Who?"

"DJ Pony."

"What? How?"

"She's Oliver's girlfriend."

Her mouth is still open with the shock of it.

"I'm living next door to DJ Pony? Me? She's there? Like, now?"

I nod.

"But how can we afford her?"

"She's doing it as a favor, for what we've got."

"That is so good. I wasn't looking forward to tomorrow morning."

"Me neither. I was going to be the dead one."

She gives my face another swipe with the cotton square. "I don't know why this isn't working."

It's working for me.

We stand there for a stretched-out second, looking at each other. It's weirdly like a *who's jumping first?* moment at the edge of a swimming pool. We both chicken out this time, babbling into each other's words as Estelle makes for the window.

Relief and disappointment, again. I wish I knew what I was doing.

"So, the tree," she says.

"We've still got to figure out how to get down the tree," I say.

I open the window and we check it out. In tree fashion, the branches are lighter the farther away from the trunk they get. So even though they brush and scratch against my window, it's the wispy end, not the weight-supporting end, that's touching.

"I was thinking maybe a rope attached to my bed and tied to the tree trunk, so we've got something to support us till we reach the strong part of the branch."

"It's quite a long way down, isn't it?" says Estelle, leaning out.

"That's what I've been talking about."

"I get it. But rope should work. Do you have rope?"

"I think there's some at the thrift store. I'll go after school."

"And I've still got to rummage for something to wear," she says, pointing to the attic.

"Have your parents said Janie can sleep over?"

"Not quite." She has an absent nibble of her left hand little fingernail. "Not at all, actually."

"Would you go without Janie?"

"No way."

"Is your mother showing any sign of thawing?"

"Can't tell. It's tougher than I expected. I might have to work on my dad, as well. I'll get clothes for you, too." She gives my hair a playful tug. "If there's anything cool enough for you up there."

I can't get to sleep. And I can't decide if I want Estelle to make it to the social or not. When I think of her dancing with unworthy disc boy, it makes me clench my teeth in anger. If this is love, it hurts. Heart and jaw both aching. The other ache is more easily dealt with.

27

"We expect you to behave legally and responsibly. Strictly no alcohol. And remember, if you don't behave there will be consequences. For a start there will be no year-nine social next year."

Doesn't Pittney realize no one could care less about what happens next year? None of us would bat an eyelid if all the year eights were slurped off the face of the earth by an alien gizzard at morning recess. If you could see thought bubbles over kids' heads, all anyone is thinking about right now is dancing, drinking, and hooking up. Some are focused on more illicit substances than alcohol, and others have nothing but hair and makeup on their minds. No one gives a toss about Pittney's sermon.

My eyes are still adjusting to the vivid spray-tan color of the transposable parentheses, who are all working their phones under desk level, confirming limousine pickup times and making final arrangements for deliveries. The one person I can see paying the slightest attention is Deeks, who is sitting to one side, lining Pittney up in imaginary crosshairs and blowing him away.

"And remember, age-appropriate behavior, please, everyone. We don't want you year nines attaching to each other like limpets."

"What's a limpet?" asks Billy, one of the taggers, genuinely perplexed.

"A marine gastropod mollusk that lives suctioned onto surfaces," says Pittney.

He looks out at the sea of blank, bored faces.

"I'm talking about pashing on, making out, hooking up," he says.

This meets with raucous noises of approval and various people yelling out things like "Yeah, that's what I'm talking about," "Go, Pit dawg," and "Free condoms at the door."

He gives up.

"Remind your parents that pickup is promptly at twelve o'clock. We don't want you all turning into pumpkins."

"What's he talking about now?" Billy asks his neighbor.

Jayzo calls out, shooting me a venomous look. "What's Cereill done about the music?"

I stand, secure in the amazing life raft I've been thrown.

"We've got DJ Pony."

There is uproar. At least half the class knows who she is. The other half just wants to scream. We're all on a hair trigger and I haven't heard that volume of whooping and whoa-ing since... ever. When they calm down Jayzo says, "Bullshit."

Estelle swivels around to eyeball him. "It's true."

The bell starts blaring like a siren, and Pittney says, "Settle down, that'll do now, homeroom's over," as everyone stampedes from the room and Jayzo glares at me with an extra load of hate bombs.

It's fair to say not much schoolwork is getting done today. Em and Oliver and a few technical types dressed in black are setting up speakers and lights in the gym, so from time to time we hear satisfyingly loud bursts of music as they do sound checks.

The transposables are in there, too, checking off lists on clipboards as stuff is unloaded from vans.

A large number of the girls leave to go to dentist or doctor (hairdresser) appointments during the afternoon.

Surrounded by the buzz, Estelle and Janie are at a fever pitch of misery that they still haven't persuaded their parents to let them have the sleepover, the essential first step of the great escape.

They have a last-resort ploy they've been hoping they wouldn't need: telling Janie's mother that it's okay with Estelle's parents and hoping she'll cave and not check the story.

"Think about it—I'll be leaving the house with a sad

face, schoolbooks, no social dress, plus already in massive trouble for Sydney. As if I'd risk it!"

"But you are," I say.

"But she wouldn't *suspect* that I would."

I give them even odds at best, but they're desperate enough to try anything.

Even though it's still uncertain that she'll even make it to the social, my guts are churning at the thought of Estelle with her date. I sweep my eyes around the playground, looking for a possible disc boy. He's probably a year above me, maybe two. They'll probably kiss and I'll probably see it, and then I'll feel like hitting him, and if I do that, Estelle will probably feel like hitting me. I'm not looking forward to any of it.

"Dan, are you okay? Are you sick?" asks Estelle at the end of the day.

Lovesick, sick at heart, sick with longing, sick of feeling confused, jealous, and hopeless.

"I'm fine," I lie. "I'll get some rope sorted. Just in case."

Of course Mrs. Nelson has rope. What doesn't she have? I get a length of rope and a rope ladder, which she says every upstairs bedroom should have in case of fire.

Then I see the shoes. I know nothing about girls' clothes, but they catch even my witless eye. "Are these new?"

"Just in today. Never been worn." She turns them around, admiring them from every angle.

The magazine browsers join in a chorus of admiration.

"Fairy shoes."

"Princess shoes."

"Cinderella slippers."

They are pale pistachio green, sewn all over with little beads in a leaf and flower pattern. They remind me of Estelle, and even though I have no idea what her shoe size is, I get them for her. Ten dollars all up including the rope and ladder. I wonder if Mrs. Nelson is giving me a special price because I used to work there, but then remember everyone seems to get special prices.

I rig the rope ladder between my window and the tree trunk. Sounds straightforward, but it's not. I tie one end of the ladder to the trunk easily enough, but it takes ages and eventual weighting with a stone to successfully chuck the other end through my bedroom window. Back inside I drag the iron bedstead to the window and attach this end of the ladder firmly to its base.

Then I climb the tree again to secure a separate length of rope a few feet farther up the trunk, leaving its two equally divided ends loose so we can hold them for balance. I have to weight the rope ends, too, because whoever uses it first has to throw both ends back to the next person. It's still potentially neck-breaking, but I try it a couple of times, being careful not to look down, and adjust it so it's as safe as possible for Estelle. And Janie.

I won't need to use it. I'm allowed to go to the social, so I get to use the stairs. When I climb down the second time, I come back in to find that Estelle has left some clothes for me to wear tonight.

She's chosen a dinner suit with satin lapels and a striped collarless shirt. I put the jacket on and check myself out in the wardrobe mirror. Not a bad fit. Not bad at all. The pants are the right length and a bit big, but okay when I put a belt on.

There's an impatient knocking at my door. What? My mother never comes into my room. She says it's better for her equilibrium not to see the mess.

"What do you think? This one or this one?" She's wearing a slip and an anxious expression, holding two hangers up for my inspection.

"I know it's not really your area, but I can't decide." She holds the dresses up again. If she wants to come into my room there is no easy way to explain why I have a ladder suspended between my window and the tree.

"I'll come and look properly if you want to try them on."

We go to her room. She puts on the first dress. It looks fine. Then she puts on the other one. That looks fine, too. This is difficult. They're clothes from our other life, dressed up and expensive-looking. It makes me realize she hasn't been wearing stuff like this for a long time. I'm used to seeing her in jeans and sweaters, and that's the way she looks most like herself to me. So I tell her and she laughs.

"Yep, I've found my level, but I can hardly wear jeans tonight."

I do a mental coin toss.

"Maybe the purple one?"

"Okay, good."

I notice her earrings—diamonds the size of peas.

"Adelaide's," she says. "Mary thinks we should share them."

"Oh, yeah? So does that mean you can sell one of them?"

I say it absently, not really thinking about money for a change, but it brings on an unexpected "serious talk," identifiable by the hushed tone and small frown.

"Dan, you know what this whole thing has taught me more than anything?"

It's a rhetorical question, so I wait patiently, hoping for a short answer. "It's not what you have, it's what you *do* that counts. We know that in theory, of course, but we have been lucky—yes, lucky—to have that theory tested. And it holds."

Maybe for her. I'd like to tell her exactly how much money I need for not-so-lucky Howard, but I shut up.

"I've had my tooth fixed today and that's certainly not wonderful for the budget, but here we are, happy, busy, both going out, surrounded by generous people. And do you know what? I'm rediscovering who I am and what I want to be doing."

"Which is what? The wedding cakes aren't exactly booming."

Oops, said it out loud. It's just going to prolong things.

"I'm not giving up on them, but I love making things for the café and then seeing people enjoying them. And talking to those people and being part of the eating and the talking and general...connectedness."

She notices what I'm wearing.

"You look lovely, darling. Very handsome. Even with that writing all over your face."

She does the misty-eyed mother smile that used to make me feel angry and smother-loved, but now I'm relieved to see it. It's like proof she is still herself under there, despite everything.

"And this has been great for you, too, Dan, although it mightn't seem that way."

No, it still feels like I've been dumped by my own father.

"You're so independent."

Not really, just doing what it takes.

"You've settled into school."

True.

"You're fit and strong."

Some would say buff.

"And looking after yourself, and Howard, so well."

If only she knew how I'm not looking after Howard.

"And you've got a job."

With crap pay.

"You're altogether a different boy from the one who moved in here and curled up in bed for days on end."

"It was cold."

"It was. But that bed was like a cocoon, and you've really...hatched."

Now I'm a moth? And that's good?

"Well...thanks."

She pats the bed for me to come and sit next to her. A peck on the cheek and that'd be a wrap, and I wasn't even in trouble. She takes my hand and writes *12 midnight* on the back of it.

"I'm trusting you to take that cake out of the oven. I mean it. Midnight. To the second."

I groan. "Stop worrying! I've said I'll do it, and I'll do it." Although I'd completely forgotten about the stupid cake, to be honest.

She nods at the hand. "Matches your face." She kisses my cheek. "Can you make yourself a sandwich for dinner?"

"Yeah."

"It's a shame Estelle isn't allowed to go to the social."

"Yeah."

"Is she upset about it?"

"Dunno."

"I saw her coming home from school with Janie, though."

"Yeah."

"So at least she's got company."

"Yeah."

"Chatty guy, aren't you?"

"Yeah, I mean no. I better get ready."

"Me too. Ali's coming in for a drink when he picks me up."

"When's that?"

"An hour or so."

I start shaving, and soon I'm brooding on the poisonous idea of Estelle's date getting ready for the big night. And of Estelle getting ready, too, right next door, right this minute, and no doubt thinking about her date.

That propels me back outside to check with Em about the playlist having no slow songs. I give her some background so she understands.

You probably already realize it's a stupid thing to ask. Em patiently points out that (a) some people might want a bit of make-out music, (b) I could possibly hook up with someone else (as if), (c) if Estelle wants to kiss someone else she can and I have to deal with it, (d) if Estelle can't see what a hotty I am with my new haircut, she doesn't deserve me (that sounds like I'm full of myself, but she said it), and (e) if you're lucky enough to get DJ Pony doing the music at your year-nine social, she calls the shots and you say thank you.

28

My mother is annoyingly mobile tonight as she zips from the kitchen to the upstairs bathroom to her bedroom—up and down the hallway, up and down the stairs. She's taking cake layers out of the oven and putting the last layer in, preparing snacky things to have with drinks, doing her hair and makeup. Singing. It's like the one night of my life I'm trying to do something sneaky and she's turned into three women. Why is she making such a big deal of someone else's dumb old class reunion? Proof she doesn't get out enough.

She knocks on my door. Again! I'm popular tonight. "Shouldn't you be going soon?"

"Soon," I call out. "I don't want to be too early."

She's right, though. It's time to go. Estelle and Janie should be here any minute. In fact they should have turned up a while ago. It's quarter past seven. Five more minutes pass. And another five. Five more crawl by and now they're half an hour late.

"Where are they, Howard?"

He sighs and settles, looking up at me as though it's all so obvious.

"It can't just be hair and makeup."

He resettles and yawns, smacks his chops a few times, and closes his eyes.

"You're right! Why don't I just call her?"

I've got no credit on my phone, so I go out to the hall telephone—it's a low-tech vehicle with the handset attached by a springy cord.

"Dan! You need to go, don't you? You should be there in case Oliver and Em need help with anything," my mother says, en route to her room.

Estelle answers. It seems that her father is in the mood for a relaxed chat with the girls.

"Why tonight? He's had fifteen years to be sociable! Don't worry, I'm going to remind him we're studying and tell him we've got hair removal plans for later," she whispers. "If that doesn't do the trick, I don't know my father. See you in five or not at all," she ends dramatically.

Estelle is halfway down the ladder and Janie looking down from the trapdoor when my mother knocks and turns the door handle.

There is no time to close the storeroom door as she steps into my room.

For no apparent reason Howard starts barking like a maniac so my mother looks down, not through to the storeroom, not over to the window. Howard is jumping all over her and wagging his tail. Because she's completely occupied with getting him to stop jumping so he won't wreck her stockings, she is bending down and stepping backward and I can jostle the three of us into the hallway without her spotting the girls. Close shave. It's as though Howard knows exactly what he's doing.

"If you don't go now, you're going to be really late."

"I'm on my way," I say, heading downstairs.

Janie must have started climbing as soon as I shut my bedroom door, because she's more than halfway down the tree by the time I get outside. But she didn't manage to get the guide ropes back to the bedroom and was afraid to keep trying because of the noise they made whacking against the wall. Apparently my mother already stuck her head out of a window once to have a look around.

By the time I get up the tree, Estelle is already climbing

across the rope ladder without the guide ropes. She's half-way over but not moving.

"Dan."

"Yes."

"You could break your neck doing this."

"All right, so I worry," I say, ready to take a bagging.

"No. You were right. You really could. I really could."

She is frozen with fear. The trouble with climbing across without the guide ropes is that it's much wobblier and you have to crawl, which forces you to look down in the plummet-to-certain-death direction.

The wind changes, swinging a cold gust through the branches, making the tree and ladder sway and pitch. A glimpse of the dark ground staggering giddily far below brings on the familiar hot and cold nausea that happens just before I faint. I will not, can not, must not let that happen.

"I'm dizzy," says Estelle. The ludicrous idea of both of us sprawled and bloody at the foot of the tree, all for the sake of getting to a year-nine dance, somehow snaps me into action.

"Don't look down," I say in a voice that sounds much calmer than it feels. "I'm going to get the ropes to you and you're going to hold on to them, and we'll get you to the trunk. It's easy from there. And you're really close."

She looks at me, trying to calm down.

I start quietly singing a song, the first thing that comes to mind: "Wild World." It's used at the end of the last episode of the first season of her favorite ever TV series, *Skins*, and I know, because of the diary snoop, that she once looked at this sequence five times in a row.

She looks surprised and fleetingly suspicious (or is that my paranoid imagining?) as she clocks the song, but she tries to join in, her voice a reedy shadow of itself, swallowed by fear. I loop the ends of the rope together and throw them to her. It's a sweet throw. She just has to reach across a couple of feet and she'll have the guide ropes in her hand. It has started to rain. Big plashy drops that make a racket as they hit the leaves.

"Come on. You can do it."

Estelle looks at me, alarmed.

"I can't unclench my hand."

"Relax. Breathe slowly."

"I'm not kidding," she says, staring mystified at the closed hand. "I'm trying. It won't undo."

I move out toward her on the rope ladder, flat on my stomach, until I can reach her hands by stretching right out. Forcing myself not to look down, I unfold her fingers and put the rope into her hand. It's as though touching the rope undoes a spell. She refocuses, gathers up both rope ends, and, holding them tightly, manages to find her balance and stand up. I'm inching my way back toward the trunk as she moves toward me hanging on to the guide ropes as though her life depends on it, which it does.

She steps onto the branch and into my arms. Safe.

Her heart pounds against my rib cage as she takes some huge, gulping breaths.

"That was massively uncool," she says.

She smiles, relieved but still shaky, and follows me down the tree.

It's hard to believe how great Estelle looks. She's chosen a dress with a straight-up-and-down shape, but it's somehow floaty, too, the sort of thing a grown-up elf might wear. No, I don't think there is such a thing, I'm trying to give a general impression. In fact, the dress looks as though it's been made to go with the shoes I got for her.

Her hair is shiny, so are her eyes. And her lips, for that matter. She shimmers.

"So, how do we look?" asks Janie, spinning around. "Freak show, or awesome?"

I think Estelle looks ethereal, otherworldly, elegant, but I settle for "awesome," for once using the word with no sense of exaggeration.

When she smiles right into my eyes, I'm breathless.

I take the satin shoes out of my pocket and hand them to her.

"I got you these."

"Dan, they're...wow—" she says, looking at them.

"You don't have to wear them. They're just from the thrift store."

"No—are you kidding? I love them."

She sits down to put them on.

"Exactly my size," she says, seeming genuinely pleased. "Sometimes it feels like you know way too much about me."

Smile. Instruct face not to assume guilty expression.

The girls leave their climbing sneakers in the garden and we head off to pick up Uyen.

By the time we get to school the girls are definitely in a party mood. Particularly Estelle, deliriously relieved as she is not to have broken her neck.

I, on the other hand, am feeling more miserable by the minute. Here we are finally, and that means Estelle's date, too, will soon be arriving.

The asphalt driveway is soaked with color as girls totter along in high-heeled shoes. Parents tell their kids to behave or to have fun, to be waiting here or there at pickup time. Girls are screaming as they run from cars trying to keep hairdos dry. Music throbs out into the night. With building hostility I watch every guy arrive, trying to assess whether he measures up as a possible date for Estelle. Not one of them does. Then Phyllis turns up, Estelle's friend from the art class where she volunteers. It stops raining, as though a switch has been flipped, and we're all going inside.

"Aren't you waiting for your date?" I ask.

"Phyl's my date," says Estelle, linking arms with her.

"I assumed you asked a guy."

"Why would you assume that?" she says airily, walking off without waiting for an answer.

Huh?

Fred and Lou arrive in time to see Estelle going in with Phyllis. Lou gives me a penetrating look.

"So, large, unexpected carpe diem opportunity arises," she says.

"Don't blow it, big guy," adds Fred helpfully.

Gulp.

"You two look stylish," I say in a feeble attempt to take the spotlight off myself.

"Thanks," says Lou.

"This was once the Gazelle's," Fred says, pointing to his suit with tragic emphasis.

"You're not saying...?"

"I, too, could become a middle-aged fat guy."

Lou looks at us with amused incredulity.

"Middle age? Middle age? We're fifteen. Who cares about middle age?" she says, dragging Fred inside.

My heart starts filling with helium as I allow myself one moment to wallow in Estelle's "why would you assume that?" Why did I? But then, why wouldn't I?

Whoever wrote the book on girls, I wish they'd send me a copy, with a full glossary of terms. I go back to "love you big time," where I've spent lots of time recently, and I know one thing for sure: I have to kiss Estelle tonight. Or die trying. I remember my stupid cake instructions. The kiss has to happen no later than twenty minutes before midnight. It seems wrong that the timing of a kiss should be dictated by a cake order. I hope it's not an omen.

Em has transformed the gym into another world. A

smoke machine has turned the floor into a drifting cloud. Lights pick up the ground and mid space only, making the ceiling disappear. The floating mist is shot through with melting colors; purples and blues morph into pinks and reds that grow orange, golden, green, and then turquoise. The colors glow, dissolve, then shatter and splinter into strobe. It's the real deal.

Trestle tables form the "bar," where the transposables are serving drinks. I look around for food but can't see any. I ask Em if she's noticed where they're serving food.

"I'm guessing it wasn't their spending priority," she says.

It's soon clear the refreshments budget has basically been spent on vodka. The transposables are busy telling people "lemon's single, orange is double, lime's triple." Shots. They've spent the whole afternoon emptying part of the contents of all the soft drink bottles and replacing what they tipped out with vodka. People can't believe their luck. The bar is being stormed.

"Is there any food?" I ask. I'm not hungry, just keen for reassurance there's some alcohol absorption on its way.

"Totally, but like way later. Gotta let everyone get their buzz on, hun," says Dannii.

"What about people who don't want to drink?" I ask.

"Yeah, like, that whole end is loser drinks," she says, waving a stencil manicure in the direction of one end of the bar.

I'm wondering whether I could get kicked out of school for this. I asked the transposables to take over refreshments, so does the buck stop with me? Probably. There's not a thing I can do about it now. Getting between my year level and the alcohol would be a suicide mission. No, it's as inevitable as an erupting volcano. I'm about to be responsible for a heavy-duty, illegal session of underage drinking. Someone might choke on their vomit and die, crowd violence could erupt, children could be conceived, and it will all be my fault. The least I'd deserve would be to get kicked out of school. But how would that mesh with compulsory attendance? Maybe they hold classes at the boys' reformatory. Is there even such a thing as a boys' reformatory anymore? Would I literally be locked up or could I attend on a sort of outpatient basis, perhaps with an electronic ankle band?

I look around for Fred and Lou, both calm types in a crisis. Unfortunately, they are already making like limpets on the dance floor and it doesn't look as though anything short of a tsunami could separate them.

So I tell Oliver about the drinks. He calmly gets on the phone and orders some cartons of bottled water to be delivered. He tells me to spread the word that they are spiked, too, thereby ensuring they'll be drunk, with any luck diluting all the alcohol swimming around.

Estelle and Janie are dancing with Phyllis and Uyen and a bunch of other girls who were at primary school together. I warn them about the amount of vodka in the drinks and remind Estelle and Janie that they can't risk getting trashed tonight, seeing as they're officially not here *and* they have to get back to Estelle's room via a ladder, making no noise unless they want to be grounded for their natural lives.

Estelle grabs me and shouts over the music, "Don't be so responsible."

"I can't help it," I shout back.

Outside I wait for the water and worry about the kiss. Would Estelle kiss someone she sees as "responsible"? Isn't that word like an official antiaphrodisiac? And if she could get past that and consider kissing me...How? When? Where? Rewind. How! How can I move on from *how*? I don't know how to kiss a girl. It's a classic learning-by-doing activity. Fred and Lou seem to have cottoned on without any trouble. How difficult can it be? And there is the crux of the matter: I have no idea how difficult it might be.

If I could only put *how* out of my mind for one moment, the *when* is also critical. If it could be quite soon, there's the potential for a good couple of hours of further kissing, assuming all goes well. That alone is reason enough to act decisively. But it's here that *where* kicks in and has to be faced. What if I make my move on the dance floor and am rejected or, worse, screw it up so badly that Estelle laughs, or is sick or something, and the whole year level witnesses my pain and/or humiliation?

From another lifetime I remember that the Latin word for *kiss*, *osculum*, is supposed to be somehow like kissing itself. I say it a few times. There's some puckering of the lips but not too much, a bit of tongue movement, but again, not too much. Who says Latin is a dead language? I decide that a slow motion and, of course, silent *osculum* has to be as good a place to start as any.

There's no sign of the water delivery truck. Damn it, I would seize the day, or the night, in this case. *How* is *osculum*. *When* is now. Right now. And *where* is wherever Estelle is when I walk back in there. My heart is thumping as though it's about to explode. But there's no going back. The adrenaline is pumping. I remind myself of her note: "love you big time." I can do it. I can.

The hot dancing throng seems impenetrable. The music warps around my jagged heartbeat. Can I really do this? I see Estelle, as though with ninja vision. I stride over, take her hand, draw her close, and kiss her. I just do it. The *osculum* is a perfectly good place to start, and Estelle takes it from there. She puts her hands on my shoulders, pulls me closer, and whispers, "About time." After some minor nose bumping, I am sinking hard into the impossible softness of the kiss, entangled and lost. After much too short a time in the middle of this best place, Em interrupts us.

"Sorry to break up the love, guys, but someone's got to be out there when the water arrives."

I have to muster all my self-control not to shout: *"Leave us alone!"* I have to remember that I owe Em my life. I have to imagine what this night would be without her amazing work.

"Okay," I say.

"I'll come, too," says Estelle. But Phyllis and Uyen arrive, ready to pull her back to the dance floor.

"I'll be straight back," I say. "You know getting cold makes you sad."

"I know," she agrees. "But..." She's wondering how *I* know. (It's on her top ten list of things that make her sad.)

I kiss her again and drag myself away.

Waiting outside, I feel delirious—light-years from my pre-kissing state of mind. I completely understand the point of kissing. No wonder Fred and Lou are stuck together as they are.

It's impossible to sit still. I feel as though I've been unstitched and remade into something that feels more like me. Walking around in the cold fizzing spring air, I'm almost pleased to be out here, to have a chance to absorb what's just happened. Something large and happy has unfolded in my chest, erupting in a smile that won't quit. I can't remember ever feeling so lighthearted. Or is my heart full? Or bursting? Not aching, that's for sure.

A pizza van arrives and two guys unload piles of flat boxes. Based on the sounds coming from inside, the food is exactly what people want.

Against the sounds of cheering, an icy hand grips me. Bam. As though I've built a flimsy partition wall in my head that comes crashing down, revealing a billboard-size fact: I have to be honest with Estelle.

I have to tell her about the diaries, otherwise everything

I'm feeling about her is a big fat lie. And I'm unworthy of her.

I've screwed up by kissing her before coming clean about it.

I've tricked her into thinking I'm someone she'd want to kiss.

Something in my head is still trying to prop the partition up. What about *what she doesn't know can't hurt her*? I try it on for size. It's crap. Who am I kidding? Of course it can hurt her. And haven't I promised myself to try to be good, whatever that means?

By the time the water finally arrives, I sign for it, get it inside, and spread the word about it being spiked, the pleasure of kissing Estelle has given way to the sure knowledge that once I tell her what I've done, I'll never kiss her again.

We see each other and as we meet up, I blurt it out. "I read your diaries."

She's speaking at the same time: "Did you read my diary?"

"Yes," I say.

"How could you do that?" She's struggling to believe it.

"I'm sorry." Words have never felt so inadequate.

"So, you opened one and saw it was a diary, and then closed it? You only read what you couldn't help seeing?"

She wants me not to be as bad as I am. She's offering me the half-truth escape card. I can seem less scummy than I am. For some reason, Howard of all people comes to mind—that serious, considering look he gives with his head cocked to one side. Have things come to this, my moral arbiter is an elderly poodle?

Apparently.

I can't sell any of us short. I can feel my heart leaving my chest, getting out before serious damage is done.

"I read them all."

The look of disappointment on her face flies up and collides with my heart on its way out the door.

She walks away.

Then turns back. "You're...you *were* disc boy."

I am:

1. Scum.
2. An idiot.
3. Unworthy.
4. Bereft.
5. Aching.
6. Brokenhearted.

29

Zero to one zillion, and back to zero in the space of one school dance.

Things could not get any worse. So I think. Wrong again. I eat some pizza with Lou and Fred, dance a bit, try to keep an eye out for Estelle, who is, reasonably enough, avoiding me. Then it's eleven o'clock, only another forty minutes to struggle through and I'll have to round them up and get them home. If they'll come.

That's when Estelle staggers back in range. She is dancing with a piece of pizza. Janie is apologetic. "She never drinks, I don't know what got into her. It's gone straight to her head."

"How much did she have?"

"Two lime drinks."

"That's six shots."

"We tried to get the ones without vodka but they all got mixed up."

"You're not drunk."

"I didn't have anything. Too scared to risk it. And she wasn't going to, either, then it was like someone pushed her moron button."

That would be me.

Estelle comes over, talking to the pizza slice.

"You idiot," I say, feeling only affection and guilt.

"Juur an idiot. And juur not a lovely boys," she says.

"How are we going to get you back like this? What if my mum's home early and you have to climb the tree? Did you think about that?"

"Think, think, think. Don't worry so mush!"

"Who's going to worry if I don't?" The story of my life.

Then while she's asking me what's the big deal, why's it my business, who am I to tell other people what they should do, she falls over.

"Do you want some fresh air?"

"Why?"

"You're pissed."

"Are not," she says. "Anyway juur a big liar and a spy and I hate you."

"Come on," I say.

She shoves me in the chest. Jayzo sees it, and it's the

invitation he's been waiting for. He comes over and shoves me, too. "Get off 'er," he says.

"I'm trying to help her," I say.

"Don't juu patronize me," Estelle says.

Someone tells us to take it outside. I don't "do" outside, in that sense, but this thing with Jayzo has been building all term and I'm not going to get out of it. I make sure Janie and Phyllis are looking out for Estelle and go outside, hearing Estelle as I go: "Give 'im a pasting." It's not clear which of us she's talking to, but I'm guessing it's Jayzo. And it's not like I don't deserve it.

The year-twelve bouncers stop anyone following us out. So here we are, just the two of us, face-to-face finally.

For a second I hope the cool night air will have a sobering effect on Jayzo, but no such luck. Even as I turn to speak to him, he swings a punch in the direction of my head. I duck and shove him down onto a bench.

"We don't have to fight," I say.

He doesn't agree. He head butts me as he staggers up. I manage to avoid the full impact, but he follows it up with an almighty shove in my chest, which pulls an involuntary "ooouf" noise out of me, just like you see in cartoon fights, as I fall in a sprawling heap.

He tries to kick me as I'm lying here on the ground, but it only half impacts as I manage to roll out of range, grabbing his legs. He falls, landing on top of me, and starts swinging random punches at close range while I struggle

and squirm my way out from under him. He lands a thud-
ding punch in my solar plexus. I clench too late to avoid
a sharp sweeping nausea. I know I have to get to my feet
or he'll be up and kicking my head within seconds. I haul
myself up, retching, while Jayzo momentarily nurses his
fist.

I stand there panting, energized by the rush of horrified
excitement and fear.

Jayzo picks himself up slowly, never taking his eyes
off me.

"Can we stop now? I don't want to fight," I wheeze.
Backing off before he kills me has to be worth one last shot.

He responds by flying at me with his full body weight,
so we both go crashing to the ground again. My shoulder
takes a fair bit of the impact and a sharp pain shoots
through it as I frantically reposition myself to swing the
hardest punch I can muster. Miraculously, it lands home,
a direct blow to the jaw, with a gruesome crunching sound
of skin, bone, vessel, tendon, all impacting way too fast,
under too much pressure. If it's hurting his face as much
as it's hurting my hand, I almost feel sorry for the guy. But
not for long.

Now he's angry. And I'm shit scared. I'm no fighter, and
I know it would only take a bit of bad luck here for me to
end up with brain damage or a broken neck.

We both struggle to our feet again and are circling each
other. I try to remember anything my dad ever told me

about fighting. Avoid it at all costs. Talk your way out of it. Run. But if you need to, here's how to throw a punch...

Jayzo's a ruckman, a lot heavier than I am. I'm a runner. My advantage is that I'm quick, and I'm sober. I'm more convinced by the second that I'd be dead by now if he weren't wasted.

"What's this about?" I ask, desperate to buy some time. "Why are we doing this?"

"'Cause you asked for it, dickhead," he replies.

As the diameter of our circle decreases, I'm buzzing, ready to spring, longing to spring. I position myself in front of the bench. As Jayzo lunges at me again, I jump sideways and he bashes his knee into the bench. Now he's roaring with fury. He charges me, swinging a fist at my head. I swerve out of his path, managing to land a solid punch in his stomach. It doesn't set him back even for a second. His next punch strikes me squarely on the left side of my face, which feels and sounds as if it's splitting in two. He makes the mistake of pausing to enjoy his handiwork, unguarded for a moment, and I take advantage of the pause. I heave my whole body, my protesting shoulder, and every weight repetition I've ever endured into that punch. It lands with a sickening crack right on his nose, which starts bubbling blood.

He sits down, groaning. We're both panting and drenched in sweat.

"Are you okay?" I ask.

A sound escapes his blood-covered lips. It couldn't be, could it? A snort of laughter?

"You wimp, you don't ask the guy you're bashing if he's 'okay,' " he says. "Don't you know anything?"

"Not really, no," I say.

I take off my shirt and hand it to him. He balls it up and sticks it under his nose.

"I'd keep going, only I'm a bleeder," he says.

"That's fine," I say. I'm alive, and it feels like a miracle.

"That was a lucky punch for a loser nerd like you," he says. "You can't fight for shit."

"I know."

While we sit, bleeding and sore, we get our breath back and talk as the music thumps on in the background and the rain starts up again.

"What exactly is your problem with me?" I blurt out.

"You're so smart, you tell me."

"You don't like that I'm smart?"

"You don't even listen. In class. But you get it all. Better than Pittney even. I can stare at it till my brain's busting."

"You're talking about math?"

He grunts an affirmative noise.

"You don't act like you care about math."

"I don't, dickhead, but I need it. For carpentry. Apprenticeship."

We talk on as the rain streams over us, washing away sweat and blood. At the end of our chat I don't know if he prefers Vegemite to peanut butter on his toast, what his ordinal place in the family is, or what his dog is called. We're not exactly pals, and I'm not exactly relaxed about the idea of Jayzo in charge of sharp tools, but this is a cease-fire, and I hear myself saying I'll help him with math. If he'd spend as much time working as he does intimidating kids and terrorizing teachers, it'd be a start.

I stand up. It hurts. Everywhere.

"Sorry about the nose," I say, pulling my sodden jacket on.

"No worse than the average footy game," he says, giving me a friendly smack where he's punched my face in.

I wince.

"Wimp," he says, smiling at me for the first time. "Tie the boot tighter."

Back inside, pizza has been eaten, water drunk, dancing done, and amazingly things look more or less the way a well-organized social might actually look. People are having fun. Great fun. Estelle greases me off on the way in, but I'm relieved to see she's fit enough to be upright and dancing. Janie gives me a sympathetic eye-roll, so I guess Estelle has not yet publicly disowned me. Time enough for that tomorrow.

The music is amazing. Everyone is up and dancing. Em has made it impossible not to be. So I dance for a while, sore, tired, rain drenched, minus a shirt. I let myself dissolve into the crush of sweating, shouting kids, jumping to one beat. And I get what I'm after, a bit of soothing oblivion.

Em settles the beat and moves into a slow-dance version of some song I don't know, but it has the effect of everyone who can coupling up and everyone else hugging and swaying in little groups. Settle-down-and-make-out music. Em makes eye contact with me, giving me a *where is she?* hands-up gesture. I shrug back and she makes sympathetic *boohoo* fists in front of her eyes. Yep, that about sums it up.

After what has got to be the shortest-ever perfect relationship on record, I have to face the cold reality—I've blown it with Estelle. I've betrayed her. She knows it. It's over. And now, despite what I imagine will be a vigorous objection, I somehow have to get her home.

30

Getting Estelle home is not easy. She's sick three times and otherwise alternating between being very grumpy and very amused.

"That pizza was off," she says. "I got pood foisoning."

"You're drunk," Janie tells her patiently for the thousandth time.

"Don't be riduckulous—redukeulous—rid*i*culous. I don't even drink. I had about two drinks. Three. Maybe four."

"Half full of vodka," I say. "Which I warned you about."

"Okay, smarty-pants," says Estelle. "Here's a newsh flash: You're not. Smart."

She spins around to Janie. "He read my diaries, an thas not nice."

"No," agrees Janie. "Dan's a bad boy."

"You'd never do tha to a friend, never—"

Janie considers. "Well, honestly, I'd be tempted. If I fancied the person, and there they were—"

"Whaddabout do to others as you would do unto you to?"

"Yeah, only I don't keep a diary, so that wouldn't apply," says Janie.

"But he was so lovely, so so so lovely. But reeeally he wasn't. He was just anotha mean old wolf in clothes," says Estelle. "He was my disc boy."

I try to believe in a time when Estelle thought I was lovely, but it doesn't feel real.

"Why disc boy?" I wonder, not really expecting an answer.

Janie takes pity. She talks girl, and decodes after a moment's reflection. "So disc equals CD equals your initials, reversed, add to that you like the same music, or she thought you did. Maybe you were just using your spy material to get into her—"

"I wasn't. It's true. We like the same music. Really."

"Yeah, I'm guessing it's not going to make much difference now," says Janie.

"Wheresh yer nice shirt I gotcha?" Estelle wants to know.

"I lost it in a fight," I say.

"Youseee! Fighting, not smart at all," she says.

Janie and I persevere. Our ten-minute walk turns into

fifteen. I'm quickly losing my safety margin. The cake will be in cinders by the time we get home at this rate.

Estelle decides to sit down for a rest. She feels tired.

I have about two minutes left before the cake has to be out of the oven. Or I will be dead. As opposed to my current state of health: three-quarters dead.

I lose it.

"Get up or the cake will burn and I'll be in the shit and it'll be all your fault."

Estelle leaps to her feet with a new sense of purpose.

"Do not burn the cake. Shoulda told us. See not so smart," she says, taking off. Janie and I run after her.

I'm hoping my mother is not home early—there's no way we'll get Estelle up the tree in this condition.

We stumble into the kitchen just as the timer bell on the oven starts to beep. Howard yowls a yawny sound, stretches out his back, wags his tail, and hobbles over to say hello.

The kitchen smells great, warm and fruity. But getting a cake safely landed with Estelle in her current state is tricky. Industrial-size cakes are extremely heavy and ten times hotter than little cakes.

So I've got the giant oven mitts on and I'm trying to maneuver the massive cake out of the oven and put it on the wooden table in one smooth action. But Estelle is right in my face.

"How could you? How could you when you're such a lovely lovely boynextdoor? That smells *really* good."

Janie corrals Estelle and I deliver the cake safely. One thing I haven't messed up.

Getting glummer by the minute, I make some coffee, hoping to sober Estelle up before the attic climb, while Janie starts moving Estelle in the direction of my bedroom—after we persuade her it's not okay to go home via the front door.

"But I've got my key," she says.

"But tonight you have to go home through the attic. Because your mum and dad don't know you're out."

When the message finally sinks in, she starts whispering.

"Don't tell *anyone anything*. Because, me and Janie, they ground us. All the time. They will *kill* us if they find out."

"That's right," I say.

"Up the tree!" she says, heading for the door.

"It's okay, my mother's not back, we're going up the stairs."

"But then they'll know," she insists, heading for the door again.

Janie shakes her head in disbelief and says quietly, "If you wanted to rethink the whole confession thing, I don't think she's going to remember much about tonight."

"I can't," I say.

"Your funeral," she says.

Estelle has somehow got hold of a knife and she lunges for the cake. Janie removes the knife in the nick of time. "Thank god you don't usually drink; I can't handle this."

Back upstairs, after we've poured as much coffee as we can into Estelle, we need equal parts of persuasion, pushing (me), and pulling (Janie) to get her up the attic ladder. Once there, she decides she should sleep in the attic, so there's some more persuading and a bit of carrying to get her back down into her bedroom. At least we get there via a properly built fold-down staircase, which Estelle then insists we fold back up, despite the fact I'm going to need it again in a couple of minutes. We humor her. It's not worth arguing when she's like this.

Her bedroom is amazing. Like the rest of her house, it looks like a magazine shoot popped into 3-D—a state-of-the-art modern opposite of her attic. She has a double bed up on a platform. One open door leads to a walk-in wardrobe, another to a bathroom.

Just as we're thinking that we've made it, unbusted, deed done, we hear Estelle's parents' voices right outside her door. We freeze, eyes locking, holding a collective breath. Estelle is shocked into alertness. Or maybe it's the coffee finally kicking in. It sounds as though Vivien has just arrived home from her opening and Peter is telling her to keep her voice down because the girls are asleep.

"Nonsense. They never settle down before midnight on a sleepover."

"I haven't heard a peep all night."

"I'll just see if they're awake..."

We think the same thought at the same time. Janie flicks off the light, and we're all under the duvet in two seconds.

As the door opens, the hallway light shines through the duvet stitching. I'm trying to breathe silently and praying that I don't sneeze. Their voices are at close range.

"Girls, are you awake?" Vivien asks in a stage whisper.

"Vivien...I told you..."

Janie manages a very plausible snoring noise, and after some shuffled tippy-toe sounds the door shuts. The voices are muffled again, but we hear Vivien saying, "I need to ask Estelle where on earth she got it."

"It can wait till morning."

They're gone and miraculously we haven't been sprung.

Estelle and Janie are in silent fits of laughter, bed-shaking, quaking, tear-streaming, snort-suppressing laughter.

"I'm going to wet my pants," Janie gasps, making a dash for the bathroom.

That leaves me and Estelle in bed together. My wildest dream come true. Two small points of difference: It smells like vomit in here and Estelle hates my guts.

I get up, pull down the stairs, and head up into the attic.

"See ya."

"Yeah, sure."

31

There's no way I can sleep now, so I go out with a flashlight and a Stanley knife to get rid of the evidence in the tree. I hiss at a couple of possums as I cut the ladder from the trunk. The guide rope I untie and wrap around my body, mountaineer-style.

When I get back to earth, clouds have cleared and the full moon cuts sharp shadows of Oliver and Em into grassleached black and white.

"Hey, 'sup, dude?" Oliver greets me. He's kidding. He has a way of doing the cool talk in quotation marks that always makes me smile. Even now.

"Thanks again for tonight. Sorry about the drinking."

"Seen lots worse," says Em. "You're the only one who

got violent, and everyone was gone by midnight. Easy gig. Dannii's brother brought his truck, and the little girls packed up the empties."

"And what's the story with you and Estelle?" Oliver asks.

"Shortest relationship in history."

"Nah, she'll be fine tomorrow."

"She'll be sober. But I won't be forgiven."

"What for?"

"You don't want to know."

"Things never look so bad in the morning," says Em.

Maybe that's true of some things, but me reading Estelle's diaries can only look worse when the sun comes up.

Underneath the hemorrhaging disaster of my problem with Estelle there's another niggle of unfinished business. I scroll: The cake is out of the oven. The girls got home undetected. There weren't any major crises at the social. Howard needs an operation, but there's nothing I can do about that except buy a lottery ticket. My mother will be home soon. By herself. That must be weird after all those years of coming home with my father...

That's it. My father. Since the deep and meaningful with Estelle, his present has been burning its way into my thoughts. I've ignored it for so long, can I really face it tonight?

I put it off.

I pull the rope ladder back in through the window and stuff it in the wardrobe.

I drag the bed back to its right spot.

I scratch Howard's ears. He twitches them, annoyed. He doesn't appreciate being used as a procrastination device.

I go to the toilet.

I have a shower and examine my injuries carefully: face, rib cage, shoulder.

I clean my teeth. At least none of them got broken, but the inside of my mouth is swollen and cut up.

I dust the present off and put it on my bedside table.

I look at it, my hands shaking. That's probably just from the fight.

It's not like it's a bomb.

I unwrap it. Inside there's a parcel and an envelope.

In the parcel there's an iPod.

In the envelope there's a letter.

Maybe it just feels like an hour that I sit with the letter on my knee, maybe it's no more than five minutes.

In the end I read it as fast as I read Estelle's diaries. I fly across the pages, swallowing scraps and gulping down paragraphs with an appetite so fierce it consumes me.

> *...understand... don't want to talk to me... pretty*
> *thick... not know... gay... I'm sorry... cold and*
> *miserable there... how could I not... somehow*
> *kept it in a different room from the rest of my life...*

how... my crazy parents... why... your mum...
best friend... loved her, still do... fun... so happy...
pregnant... so this is how it unfolds... both so
excited... dear little you... best thing ever... you're
cool with... different sexuality... lie... more like not
the whole truth... our relationship... always true...
cracking my heart... you might be feeling... let
down... embarrassed... like I'm a big phony loser...
not that simple... your nice life... move schools...
good thing... how I lost the family fortune...
too much debt... my mistakes... idiot... people I
trusted... I let a lot of other people down... whenever
you're ready... understand... time... I love you...
under the anger... you know it... mum not too
thrilled... best for all of us... music for you...

I start breathing again, slow myself down. The letter ends:

None of this is offered as an excuse, Dan, but I hope
it starts to be an explanation. I need to talk to you, so
call me when you're ready, even if it's just to yell at
me. Any contact will be welcome.

We're going to be fine, all of us. We just need to find
a new shape.

Love from
DadXXXOOO

I've missed him so much.

I get into bed and read his letter through three times slowly. It bangs me over the head with some of the things I love most about him—honesty and confidence and affection and humor.

Rummaging under the bed, I find the diary I kept when we first moved in here, and on the last page, the list of things I'd thought impossible.

32

The list, again:

1. Kissing Estelle. Unbelievable, but it happened. And I can remember every moment. It'll never happen again.
2. Getting a job. Done. It's not like I've made anything like the amount of money we'd need as a safety net if *I Do* Wedding Cakes folds, but we're getting by. And I know how to wipe down a table. It was a bit of grandiose mad anxiety if I really thought it was up to me to support us.
3. Cheering my mother up. Didn't I even realize that how she feels is up to her? I helped her find a job and she's started cheering herself up.

4. Not being a loser at school. Turned out to be possible, with lots of help. I've just organized the year-nine social. Thanks to Em it was great. Thanks to Oliver I've got non-loser hair and clothes. Thanks to my fear of getting beaten up, I'm fit and strong. I haven't fainted in a while. I've fought Jayzo and survived triumphant as his math tutor. Hmmmm.

5. Talking to my father. He'll be here in three weeks. Still scary, but definitely not impossible.

6. Being good. As opposed to my father. What a judgmental little git. I've lied now twice to help friends do what they wanted to do, stuff I figured they were entitled to do. I've pinched clothes from school lost property. I've eavesdropped on my mother and her friends trying to find out what the hell was going on in our life. I listened in on Estelle and Janie when they were talking about me. I read *Estelle's diaries*, desperate to get to know someone I decided I loved before I even met her. Then I read them *again*! Good? I figure the best I can do is sort things out on a case-by-case basis as I stumble along.

33

The iPod is charged and loaded with a playlist—"songs for Dan." My dad has written down the song titles and why he likes them. The first one is from way back when he was my age: "Walking on the Moon" by the Police. Giant steps.

As I listen, I realize I have to go up to the attic one last time. There's something I need to give Estelle. No excuses, just the beginning of an explanation.

I climb the ladder and sit at her desk in the attic for a long time, deciding what my note should say. In the end I write just one line. And finally I can haul my aching body to bed.

»«

I wake swinging from a tree, tied by one foot, trying to free myself so I can get to the church and stop the bell so Estelle and Janie can get out of the elevator in time...But the bell pushes insistently through layers of consciousness. It's our doorbell, a Big Ben chime.

I jump out of bed, forgetting about the fight, and feel my face, my shoulder, my back, and every rib screaming out their protest as I limp to the window and open the curtain, trying to figure out what time it is. It looks early. I pull on some track pants and a sweater, stop in the bathroom to reassure myself that the Sharpie scrawls disguise the worst signs of the fight—kinda—and head downstairs, starving.

Ali is in the kitchen. I barely have time to register this bizarre fact when my mother comes in, leading Vivien.

We've been busted, after all.

Now I'll have to face the music for sure. All those false assurances I made about being a responsible friend...I meant them at the time.

I look down at my grazed hands. How am I going to explain this?

"How do you explain this?" asks Vivien.

But her tone is all wrong. She's curious, excited. I look up. My mother is calmly pouring coffee. Vivien is peering into the palm of her own hand.

"Seriously, where did you find this?" she asks.

I feel like hitting my own head like they do in cartoons to see if I'm hearing properly. Shouldn't she be demanding to know why I've disobeyed her specific instructions and helped Estelle defy her ban?

She is holding out her hand. In it is the little carving I gave Estelle.

"Adelaide left it to me," my mother is saying, handing around the coffee.

"It's museum-quality netsuke. I would have borrowed it to put in the exhibition if I'd known about it," says Vivien.

"But how come you've got it?" my mother asks.

"Dan, you gave it to Estelle. Is that right?" says Vivien.

"Er, yeah."

What's Ali doing here? Wearing a suit? He offers me some toast. I take it.

"When I came home last night there it was, sitting on the kitchen table, on Estelle's book. I said to Peter, "Where on *earth* did this come from?" and he said it was Estelle's, and I went straight up, but the girls were asleep, of course. Anyway, it's very exciting."

"There are lots more," says my mother.

Vivien's eyes widen with excitement. "You do realize they're worth a fortune?"

My eyes widen with excitement.

"They're ancient Japanese belt ornaments," she says. "Carved ivory."

"Really?" says my mother. "We must have at least a dozen."

"Sixteen, counting that one," I say. "But that's Estelle's."

Vivien hands it to me. "It certainly is not. It's much too valuable to give away."

Maybe Ali had too much to drink and my mother let him sleep on the sofa. Yeah, that must be it.

Vivien gets up.

"Let me know if you want to sell them and I'll put you in touch with a reputable auction house. They should be auctioned internationally if you want a good price."

But I'm pretty sure Ali doesn't drink. So what gives?

"Thanks, Vivien. When you say a fortune...?"

Howard looks up, alert to the conversation, waiting for us to remember the big op.

"If the others are this good, there'll be enough to give yourself a nice long holiday, not worry too much if the business doesn't work out, and heaps left over."

My mother sits down abruptly.

Ali stands, kisses my mother on the top of her head(!), and says, "Time for me to open up."

He leaves. He just kissed my mother?

Vivien stands, ready to head off, too.

"Meanwhile, you should insure them, and get them stored somewhere safe," she says.

"Good idea," says my mother.

My mother and I sit in stunned silence for a minute or two.

"Howard needs an operation," I say.

"I know."

"I didn't want to worry you," we say at the same time.

"I took him to the vet. I've been trying to put some money aside for it, but then my stupid tooth…" She starts crying. And it's possible to put my arms around her again and give her a hug.

"I'm not sad, Dan, just relieved. I'm hopeless at the wedding cake business. I've got rid of more clients than you can imagine. And this means I can ditch it. Thanks for taking that out, by the way," she says, nodding in the direction of the midnight cake. "How was last night?"

I nod. "Okay. What about you?" I notice she is still in her going-out clothes. "Was the reunion good?"

"It was. I haven't quite made it to bed. Ali and I sat up talking all night. We decided we can probably manage to work together and go out."

Say *what*?

She is smiling as she registers my double take. She looks younger, and pretty, and very tired.

"Is that going to be too weird for you?"

"I…no. I mean, yeah, but I guess not."

"I need sleep. And you look like you could do with some more, too," she says.

How can she be this calm? Maybe she's just stunned, like me.

And I've had all of about three hours, so I don't argue.

I shut my bedroom door and lean my forehead against it. My mother and Ali? My mother and anyone? I try to make the adjustment. It's not like, in the circumstances, she and my dad are going to get back together.

I'm distracted by the horrible thought that I've lost track of exactly where the box with the netsuke is. I find it in the bottom of the wardrobe and leave it there. It's not till I turn around that I notice a sleeping girl in my bed. A sleeping girl in striped pajamas, snoring softly.

34

Someone's been sleeping in my bed and she's still there. I touch her hand and she opens her eyes straightaway and sits up with a small groan.

"I didn't sleep much last night," she says.

"Neither."

"I was sick some more, then I had a shower, then I went up to the attic, the land of feeling better, and I found these on my desk." She is holding my diary and the note I left her.

"I don't expect you to think it's okay, just because I let you read my diary, too," I say.

"Janie says I was obnoxious last night. I'm sorry."

She's apologizing to *me*?

"She said you were patient and determined to get me home safely, no matter how much I abused you. Heroic, she said."

Janie was defending me to Estelle?

"I wouldn't go that far."

"I'm sorry to hop in, it was so warm," she says.

"You're welcome."

"You kissed me."

"I did."

"That seemed...What made you do that—so suddenly?"

I shrug. "I needed to kiss you."

"I thought I was going to have to kiss you first. I thought you were too shy."

"I reminded myself of your note."

"What note?"

"This note," I shuffle around my desk. It's not there.

"Do you mean this note?" She's holding it, too. "I was going to write on the back of it, but I fell asleep instead. How come you kept it?" She reads it aloud, puzzled: "'I owe you big time'?"

I owe you big time? Not "love you big time"? I *owe* you?

A meteorite-size "d'oh" hurtles toward me and lands on my head. I've misread her handwriting. At least a thousand times over.

I decide not to share my mistake just yet.

She looks again at the note. "I always put kisses and hugs on. I'd call that mild encouragement."

"I guess that was all I needed."

Then she unfolds my note to her. My one-line note. My make-it-or-break-it note.

"So I read this," she says. "Then I read your diary." Her eyes fill up with tears. She's sad, for me. "The whole holidays...it was like a—furniture catalog. So I could kind of understand, just a bit, how you did what you did."

I hand her a tissue and she blows her nose.

My note said, *I was so lonely.*

But I'm not anymore.

35

"My mum told me about the loot. How are you going to spend it?"

"Howard's operation, for a start."

He gives a sleepy tail thump.

"You've been rescued by Adelaide."

"Yeah, but we'd already started rescuing ourselves, more or less."

"Do you want to go out with me, Dan?"

"You know I do. But do you want to go out with me? After what I did..."

She gives me the longest look, holds out her hand, and I sit next to her.

"There are two things. First, I don't think you were

yourself—you were sad and lonely. And second, you're the only person I want to tell all that stuff to anyway. No, there are three things. That list in the back of the diary— you put kissing me on the top." She smiles her mile-wide smile. "Good call."

She leans against me, resting her head on my shoulder like it's been there a thousand times. I bend down and kiss the top of her head. Her hair smells like lemons. She looks up at me and I kiss her again. She breaks away, gazing at my face. "Do you think you'll ever get that ink off?"

ACKNOWLEDGMENTS

Heartfelt thanks to Greer Clemens, Kaz Cooke, Claire Craig, Katelyn Detweiler, Jack Godsell, Jill Grinberg, Philippa Hawker, Julia Heyward, Catherine Hill, Simmone Howell, Penny Hueston, Farrin Jacobs (and the Little, Brown team), Julie Landvogt, Nigel Langley, Louise Lavarack, Violet Leonard, Angus McCubbing, Joel Naoum, David Parsons, Cheryl Pientka, Jenny Sharp, George Wood, Zoe Wood, and especially Jamie Wood.

And for wonderful places in which to write, thanks to Varuna, the Writers' House, for the Eleanor Dark Flagship Fellowship, to Iola Mathews, Writers Victoria, and the National Trust for the Glenfern Writers' Studios, and to the Readings Foundation for the Glenfern Fellowship.

For more from Fiona Wood,
don't miss *Wildlife*.

Turn the page for a sneak peek!

Available Now

In the holidays before the dreaded term at my school's outdoor education campus two things out of the ordinary happened.

A picture of me was plastered all over a massive billboard at St. Kilda junction.

And I kissed Ben Capaldi.

At least twice a year, my godmother, who is some big-deal advertising producer, comes back to Melbourne from New York to see her family and people like us, her old friends.

Her name is Bebe, which is pronounced like two bees, but we call her Beeb.

She doesn't have kids, so I get all her kid attention,

which to be completely honest is not a huge amount. But it's "quality time." And quality presents. Especially when I was little. When I was five, she arranged for me to adopt a baby doll from FAO Schwarz. She took photos of me in the "nursery"—they actually had shop assistants dressed up as nurses—and I showed them at school.

That was when I started being friends with Holly. As she looked at my doll, Meggy MacGregor—who had a bottle, nappies, designer clothes, a birth certificate, and a car seat—I could see her struggling. It was jealousy/hatred versus admiration/envy, and lucky for me admiration/envy won the day. Holly's a good friend but a mean enemy.

We were at the beach house, lounging around in a delicious haze of lemon poppy-seed cake and pots of tea, talking about digging out the wet suits for a freezing cold spring swim, and whether sharks have a preferred feeding time. I was lying on the floor, with my feet up in an armchair. Toenails painted Titanium—dark, purplish—drying nicely.

I'd just put down *Othello* for a bout of Angry Birds. My sister, Charlotte, thirteen going on obnoxious, was laughing too loudly at a text message, no doubt hoping one of us would ask her what was so funny. Dad was doing a cryptic crossword. Mum was answering e-mails on her laptop even though she was supposedly on holiday. "Sexually transmitted diseases never sleep," she said when I reminded her of the holiday concept. Gross.

She used to be a regular doctor, but she kept getting more and more obscure qualifications and went into community health and health policy, and now she basically runs the Free World from the Sexually Transmitted Infections Clinic in Fitzroy.

If you can think of a more embarrassing place than STIC to visit your mum at work, think again, because there isn't one.

Holly loves it. We went there after school on the last day of term for emergency gelato money so we'd have the necessary energy required to trawl Savers, and this old woman gave us the foulest look when we hit the street. Holly deadpanned her: "At least we're getting it treated."

Beeb was sitting on the comfy sofa, with the beautiful Designers Guild paisley fabric that she bossed Mum into choosing about ten years ago, all the bright colors now softly worn and faded, flipping through some modeling agency "books" online and saying, "Insipid, insipid, dreary, tarty, bland, blah, starved, insipid . . ." She groaned and stretched out her black-jeans-clad legs. "Where are the interesting gals?"

"They broke the mold after you two," my dad said. Meaning Beeb and Mom. It never works when my dad tries to give a compliment; he's simply not that charming.

"Thanks," I said, thinking *interesting* is after all a modest claim.

I must have sounded way more offended than I felt, because when I glanced up from my screen all eyes were upon me. Upside down, disconcertingly, because of me lying on the floor. When I untangled my legs and sat up, it was as though I'd surrounded myself with flashing lights and arrows. Everyone kept looking at me. Really looking. And I was wishing I'd just shut up, because my mother was probably about to remember that I still hadn't unloaded the dishwasher and if I had time to lie there playing Angry Birds—which is quite a distant rung on her almighty hierarchy of tasks from Reading a Required Text for Next Term—then I certainly had time to unload the dishwasher, and I had to remember the family was a community, and in order for a community to function...

Beeb got up. "Come here, kid," she said, leading me to the window. She was looking at me with a strange frown-and-squint gaze. "What did you do with all those pimples?"

"Roaccutane," I said. "I had dry skin, dry eyeballs, and no spit."

"Till they corrected the dose," said Dr. Mother.

"What about all the hardware in your mouth?" asked Beeb.

"Off last week." I ran my tongue over my teeth. They still felt weirdly slippy.

"Take off your glasses."

I did.

"You are gorgeous. How did I not notice this?" It was a eureka moment, she said later.

"Maybe because you see my visage in my mind," I said, mangling a bit of *Othello*.

"That is true, my sweetie," said Beeb.

"She has a pointy nose exactly like a witch," said Charlotte.

"Her nose is fine," said my father, who never seems to realize *fine* is as good as an insult.

"If you like huge noses, which no one actually does," said Charlotte.

"She's got character," said Beeb. "And that's what I'm looking for."

"You're talking about *her*? My sister? Sibylla Quinn?" said Charlotte, her voice squeaking with growing incredulity. "She's totally fugs. Totally."

"Don't use that word," said my mother, who only recently found out what *fugs* meant, and then only because she used it, so I felt that I had to tell her, and she said, Oh, that's disappointing. I thought it was like a cuddly version of ugly. No surprise this is the same woman who thought *lol* meant "lots of love." It was her all-purpose sign-off for texts till I set her straight a few years ago.

"I don't want pretty little generics; I want different; I want individual!" said Beeb.

"What for?"

"Perfume launch. A billboard and magazine campaign. *Jeune Femme Sauvage.*" She was rummaging in her latest designer version of the magic bag that contains her whole office. She pulled out a camera, took some photos of me, and studied the screen. "Perfect. God, you look like your mum."

"Old and tired? Poor girl," said my mother.

We looked at her. She has a high forehead and a bony nose and a big mouth. (In both senses.) She doesn't dye her hair. It's cut straight and parted on one side. It's the same color as mine. Mouse. Only she calls it rat because she's *so* funny. She does have a great smile. And she smiled.

"Take a picture. It'll last longer," she said.

Beeb took a picture of me and Mum together. We're both smiling. And I can see that even though I'm not old and tired, we do look pretty similar.

Mum hugged me and whispered in my ear: *"Dishwasher."*

friday 28 september
After Fred...

saturday 29 september
After Fred died...

sunday 30 september
After Fred died I divided my time between blind disbelief, blank chaos, and therapy.

The psychiatrist, Esther, said, Write a journal, Lou, how
about writing a journal, would you consider writing a journal, Lou, give it some thought...

We are in the slowly unwinding transition out of therapy

in the lead-up to me going away to school. Who knew: you can't just walk out of therapy. At least it is not recommended that you just walk out of therapy. No matter how many times you might keenly wish to just walk out of therapy.

There will be a formal handover to the school counselor, whose name I don't know yet. I'll be the new girl, starting in term four. Boarding for a whole term, a whole nine weeks, in the wilderness.

I've been angry through the whole therapy thing, which might be a displacement of my guilt/sorrow/depression at the whole Fred thing. We don't use *depression* in the usual sense, because truly, if I don't have a reason to feel depressed, I don't know who...

It is possible that Esther, who is after all a psychiatrist-with-a-special-interest-in-grieving-and-its-effects-on-mental-health-in-young-people, is right about writing a journal.

So I have decided, well, why not write something down?

If you don't want to write about your Feelings, you can simply write about the Physical World, what you see, what you hear...facts, things, stuff. Jeez, so it's not compulsory to eviscerate myself? To slash myself to a slow death with a million small paper cuts? Thank you kindly.

There are whole nights I do nothing but wait. For what?

You could say I have been spending too much time alone for too long. Perhaps it is indeed time to start talking to an exercise book. The internal, external...infernal, diurnal, eternal journal. It is essentially just more talking to myself, but that is okay because my heart is its own fierce country where nobody else is welcome.

Cut him out in little stars. Hard to believe a man even wrote that; it's so fragile.

I completely get that giddy arrogance, the infatuation. The laugh-and-spin embrace of the absent beloved. If you were writing an essay, you'd probably yarp on about the way in which it can be read as prefiguring Romeo's death. A portent.

I love the staccato it-t-t-teration and the soft fading sibilance of *stars*. Imagine the words breathed out, written down fast and hard onto thick, smeared paper, the tarry smell, black sputtery ink. Such potent meaning inside so delicate an image feels risky, implosive, cataclysmic.

But if there's no danger, no risk, it's not love, is it?

I've told Esther exactly nothing of any of this.

Fred and I talked about it like we talked about everything, and decided we were too young to have sex. Then we basically went for it.

Because, sure, head was saying, *Maybe not such a good idea*, but soul was saying, *I know you*, and body was saying, *Come to me*. And that's two against one.

Hey, at least we were older than Romeo and Juliet.

Fred did the research. Ever the scientist. The failure rate for condoms mostly relates to misuse, or accidents. We decided we'd go straight to a morning-after pill in the case of an accident. We also decided we wouldn't have accidents, and we didn't. We took it in turns to buy the condoms. Nowhere too near home.

Going on the pill would have meant horrible discussions. My mothers being very responsible and ultimately *understanding* and *tolerant* with about three million warnings and provisos. And the family doctor. Gag. I did not fancy the whole gang metaphorically standing at the bedside. A strange doctor would have been possible, but weird, too. I didn't need the lecture.

Condoms sometimes break because someone is being rough, or the girl isn't ready, which sounds so sad. Sounds more like rape than sex to me. That wasn't us. We were all liquid aching and longing. It was fun being beginners together. You only get that once. It took a little while. We were learning a new language, after all.

If we'd ever asked for a weekend away together, all the parents, including Fred's stepmother, would have been frowning and conferencing and counseling.

But all we asked was to do our homework together a couple of times a week, and hang out a bit on the weekend. So it was easy. And we did homework, our nerdiness as compatible as our lust. We were pretty lucky. You'd have to say.

Next week I am heading off to a jolly outdoorsy camp called Mount Fairweather, where you learn to be jolly and jolly well fend for yourselves and run up a jolly mountain and learn which way's north and how to make a fire and incinerate some jolly marshmallows, no doubt.

Esther says it will be good for me. She says it will do me the world of good. But where is the world of good? I'm pretty sure it's not stuck up a mountain with a bunch of private-school clones.

Dan and Estelle and Janie are all on exchange in Paris. They left last week. More tears. More scattering.

Dan's shrink said it would be good for him. Maybe he said *the world of good*. Perhaps Paris is the world of good.

I do try to live in the moment, but it doesn't work particularly well.

In the wall is the window. On the window is the curtain. Through the window is the moon. You can even write gibberish in the journal if you like; it still connects you to the page, to the idea, at least, of communicating. Apparently.

Sometimes I'll write to you, Fred; sometimes I'll write to me. Sometimes I will just write what I see, because *when I see a fingernail moon in fading sky* . . . I see it for you, too.